The Legendary

Barons

A Novel

I0659179

by

Michael J. Vaughn

John P. Rutledge, Editor

FIRST EDITION
2003

For David Booker and Darin Price, brothers-in-arms.

the men in fashion glasses don't understand
the game is cloth on dirt
no fred astairing into third but a
decrescendo sled across the gravel
one hand cupping the perfect white corner

– from *batbeat*, by Michael J. Vaughn
(first published in *Yarrow)*

ONE

Signing Off

It was the windbreaker that did it.

Tommy Folgett was conducting his usual post-loss lecture about concentration and focus, rooted in the belief that you could will yourself to win softball games. My beleaguered teammates were taking it in stride. They had lost; they deserved a talking-to. I, however, had a philosophical bug up my butt.

"…so let's come back here next week, get here early, and really focus on winning. Yeah, Honus?"

"Tommy, I think we've got a problem with the yelling during tough innings. All it does is get us more uptight than we already are."

Tommy can be a little dense sometimes, but I think he knew at whom I was directing my complaint. Early in the game, our defense was suffering one of those contagious butterfinger innings. After four errors and seven runs, Tommy stood up from his catcher's position to pour a little salt in the wounds.

"Come on, goddammit! Let's concentrate out there! Get your heads out of your butts and let's get an out!"

Oh, yeah – that helps. I could feel sphincters tightening all across the diamond. The next ball came to my right, and in my overly ardent desire to attain the precious out, I stiff-armed my throw to third. The ball skipped past Gilly's glove and into the dugout. Five errors, eight runs. I strolled unapologetically back to short, leveling a death stare toward home plate.

And now that stare was coming back, courtesy of Tommy's steely blues.

"I don't really want to talk about it now, Honus. I've been dealing with a lot of personal shit lately, and I just don't want to talk about it."

"Fine," I said. "Later." I picked up my bag and left, congratulating myself on a smooth signoff. Then I realized I had forgotten the windbreaker – a top-of-the-line Columbia that a friend had sent me from Tacoma. It was on the bleachers, right next to Tommy, who was lighting up his post-game cigarette.

Leaning over to retrieve the jacket, my head so close to Tommy's ear, it was too damn tempting to tack on a postscript.

"Yaknow, Tommy, I don't even like coming out here anymore."

No way Tommy Folgett could leave a comment like that unanswered. He, the master bluffer, the skinny kid from Detroit who would trash-talk opponents twice his size. Once again, the steely blues, the open-faced deadpan.

"So why don't you stop coming?"

What once would have seemed a threat, now seemed like the sweetest of invitations.

"Sure," I said. "Seeya."

And I was gone, wishing cheery goodnights to my unaware teammates, stopping to compliment the opposing center-fielder, striding the wide front path of the Double River softball complex.

After ten years, I was no longer a member of the legendary Barons softball team.

TWO

Instant Hero

My road to the Barons began at an auto credit company in Sunnyvale, California. I worked in the mailroom, and although my peon status was voluntary (leaving more brainpower for writing), I was glad when we started a company softball team. Here was a place I could shine.

I loved the game, and whenever I played it, I played my ass off – post-work batting practice, Thursday night playoff game, it didn't matter. Even when little else was going on in my life, I could always play softball.

Our first-year experience was pretty standard – namely, we stunk up the joint. In our second year, however, we demonstrated a remarkable learning curve. We practiced a lot, began to actually look like we knew what we were doing, and even sprouted some characters. Like Scary Carrie, our token female outfielder, who never looked like she was going to catch the ball but always did. Or "Spokane Sam" Heimerringer, a former high school star who had to have three beers before he could stomach playing with us. We proceeded to win the Sunnyvale co-ed trophy, along with 15 medium T-shirts that fit maybe three people on the team.

Cheering from the stands that championship night was Sarnah, an exotic beauty (I was guessing East Indian) from the collections department. I didn't really know Sarnah, but thanks to a mutual friend I knew a lot about her. She had married young, to an older man, a man with a drinking problem. I remember catching a glimpse of their photo on Sarnah's desk, and thinking that they looked happy together, that he looked like a nice guy.

By the time of our championship, Sarnah's husband had dried out, joined Alcoholics Anonymous, even started his own men's softball team. He joined her at the game, and asked her about the company shortstop – out there flinging his body at ground balls like they were hundred-dollar bills. A few weeks later I got a call – and that was Tommy Folgett.

"Hi, Honus. Yeah, hey, I saw you playing on the company team a couple weeks ago, and I was really impressed. You're quite a hustler! Listen, I got a couple of playoff games comin' up and I'm short on players. I was wonderin' if you'd like to fill in for us."

A few days later, I showed up to the impressive, ten-field Double River softball complex. Tommy gave me an extra-large T-shirt with the name "Barons" spelled out in Gothic letters, and introduced me to a bunch of guys whose names I would spend the rest of the day trying to remember.

Being an emergency sub is a beautiful thing. You've already saved everybody's butts just by showing up. If you show any actual talent, you're an instant hero.

I filled in for their right-fielder, whose jaw had met up with an errant throw the week before. The wind was blowing straight to left, so no one was much interested in hitting anything my way. I fielded one bloop single, and did a damn fine job of relaying it to the second baseman, ten feet away.

At the plate, however, I came up in the middle of a tight semifinal game and smacked a two-run double, a rising liner that shot over the left-fielder's head. Bam! Instant hero. It sparked a long rally, and we won the game. Then we won the final, and we were champions.

We spent the rest of the day consuming pizza, taking photographs and drinking beer (for Tommy, iced tea). I pushed through the turnstiles of the Double River entrance, an orange sun setting over the landfill, and tucked my trophy in the crook of my arm. I had just found myself a softball team.

THREE

An Ode to Shortstop

For all of my adult life I had played shortstop, so my relegation to the Barons' outfield was a little jarring. Especially when I saw the incumbent.

Brick Paulson was about as elegant as his first name. He was built like a linebacker, had a range of three feet to either side, and had trouble bending all the way over to field grounders. Despite these hindrances, he took every opportunity to be a showboat (like flipping the ball with his glove when it wasn't necessary), and did nothing to direct his fellow defenders. Worst of all, he wore shorts. No infielder has any business wearing shorts.

Much as I tried to be a good sport, my competitive nature sometimes got the best of me. I didn't say anything, but the body language was unmistakable, and one day Tommy pulled me aside before a game.

"Yeah, Honus, hey, I just wanted to talk to you about shortstop. I've seen you play, of course, and I know what you're capable of. But we have a certain way of handling these things. Brick's been with us from the start, and contributes a lot as a hitter, so I don't want to take him out of position mid-year. We also just won a championship, so frankly I don't want to mess with the team chemistry. What I'd like to ask of you is to have patience, and come spring training I'll throw it open for competition. I got a hunch you'll do just fine."

It worked out even better than that. The following March, when Brick saw how his teammates responded to the new shortstop, he gracefully reassigned himself to right field.

It was the last graceful move he made, because my first impression was correct: Brick was an asshole. He may have had a beautiful off-field power stroke, but he also had one of those dumbass mullet haircuts and a horrible temper. We learned to cover our heads when Brick popped out, because he would often fling his bat into the dugout, ricochets and skull fractures be damned. We were beginning to develop an unofficial Barons code of conduct, and Brick looked more and more like an endangered species.

It didn't concern me much, because I was back in my favorite spot on Earth – halfway between second and third, ten feet behind the baseline, poised for action.

I enjoyed the fact that I was good at shortstop, but what I enjoyed more were its complexities and geometric variations. The position is a Rubik's Cube of variables – outs, baserunners, types of hit balls – that spit out new and weird results on a regular basis.

I sometimes wondered if these weird things happened too often, if they were brought on by the way I fielded my position – like a hockey goalie, or a French hog rooting for truffles. One season, I tried to play in a more traditional style – back near the fringe of the outfield, trying to stay on my feet more. It was a complete failure.

So I went back to playing in the dirt, and I developed some standard plays. One was the headlong dive over the middle, followed by the backhand flip to second. Another was a slide into the hole between myself and third, then a throw to first from the knees (sometimes, the butt). But these were plays where I pretty much knew where I was going. Other times, I had to improvise.

My first trick was inspired by Tony Phillips of the Oakland A's. Diving over the middle one night, I ended up flat on my stomach, facing centerfield, the ball in my throwing hand. So I did what Tony had done – flipped the ball over my shoulder, like a bride tossing a bouquet. I turned to see Johnny Silva standing on second, the ball in his hands. The baserunner jogged back to the dugout, shaking his head.

Another, similar play was less copycatting than sheer desire. This time I ended up facing left-center with my body parallel to the baseline. What's more, my only play was to first. So I performed an earthbound barrel roll, deploying my arm as a kind of catapult. Amazingly, it worked.

My favorite play earned its status because I thought it up long before I actually used it. In hardball, when a shortstop goes into the third-base hole, he generally has enough time to spin and throw the ball to second. Not so in softball; the basepaths are much shorter, so the runners get there much faster. Finding myself in the ideal position one night – in the hole, on my knees, my back square to second base – I gave my invention a try, hopping to my feet as I hiked the ball between my legs. The ball took one long skip into Johnny's glove. The baserunner arrived a step later, looking extremely surprised.

FOUR

The Flip and The Fall

We don't really remember things in chronological order. We recall them in distilled images, snapshots filed away in our minds. If you asked me to sum up the Barons, I would refer to two of these memories. I call them The Flip and The Fall.

The Flip came after a championship game with the Bisons, an aptly named squad of beefeaters who finished the season 11-0 while serving up the only scar on our 10-1 record. During the final, the lead ping-ponged back and forth several times. We arrived at the bottom of the final inning clinging to a two-run lead. We quickly got two outs – the second a beautiful back-running catch by our left-center fielder, Stevie Becker.

Tommy walked the next guy, just to make things interesting, but I didn't care, because the next ball was coming to me. I was begging for it, cursing under my breath: "Come on, asshole, hit it to me. You know you're gonna hit it to me." When you're that ready for a ball, the rest is pretty easy: guy hits a liner, you slide to the right on your knees, the Barons explode.

I tossed my glove into the air and we had a good old-fashioned melee. But the memory didn't come till later, when we were watching the video. There in the foreground was 40-year-old Alby Thompson, the Michael Jackson of pitch-taking, celebrating the final out by turning a half-cartwheel, half-somersault across the infield dirt. The enormity of his joy demanded nothing less.

The Fall was not so joyous, but over the years it provided much more amusement. It also came during a playoff game, and was delivered by our team braggart, Rico Carlo. Rico could never quite match his own self-billing, but did piece together one MVP season through a remarkable string of bloop hits and seeing-eye singles.

On the fateful day, he was stationed in right field, and sorely underestimated the opposition's left-handed slugger. When the batter connected on a long drive, Rico turned on his short legs and ran straight back, eyes fixed firmly on the ball. He might've caught it, too, if it hadn't've been for the fence.

Again, the full effect is best appreciated on video. Rico strikes the wooden advertising panel with a thwack!, and seems to dangle there, illustrating certain refutations of the laws of gravity posited by Road Runner cartoons. Then he falls to the warning track in a heap.

None of this would be funny had Rico been seriously injured (in fact, he managed to take his next at-bat, before retiring with a bruised lip and a headache). But viewing The Fall became a pivotal event at post-season parties (and, for the rookies, an object of near-obsessive fascination). I can still picture Stevie Hammer, fresh out of high school, hitting the rewind button again and again, exclaiming, "That is just... brutal!"

To his credit, Rico took this ridicule as its own brand of fame, and realized that The Fall illustrated not just astonishing failure but great and fearless desire.

FIVE

Making Out the Lineup

The following squad of players may never have actually set foot on the same field together – over ten years, even the most stable of teams goes through dozens of changes. This is, nonetheless, the way I picture them. I have omitted right field, which, true to the tradition of Lucy Van Pelt, played host to a long list of castoffs and fill-ins.

Pitcher – Tommy Folgett

Playing a position that doesn't really make much of an impact, anyway, Tommy was not particularly talented. He didn't throw knuckleballs, he didn't throw spinners, he didn't vary speeds or change the heights of his pitches. But he did have an ability to place the ball left and right, a high arc that drew a lot of fly balls, and a low frequency of walks.

He could also be a real prick, using a variety of pitching mound dances to throw off the batter's rhythm. If you were susceptible to such antics, this could prove irritating. And if you attempted to foil him by calling timeouts, he would one-up you, backing off the rubber and toying with the ball like he was considering what to have for dinner after the game.

You would think these syncopations would throw off his fielders, but actually it was just the opposite. Never quite knowing when Tommy was going to deliver the ball, we learned to stay on our toes – which, in the long run, made us better fielders.

In the batter's box, Tommy was aware of his weaknesses and worked hard to minimize them. He had no power whatsoever, so he learned to hit the ball through the middle, where the percentages were in his favor. (If opposing teams ever paid attention, they would employ the Tommy Shift we used in batting practice, placing our middle infielders three feet to either side of second base.) Tommy also had the wisdom to bat himself last in the order, voiding any charges of managerial egotism and giving himself more time to fill out the lineup card at the beginning of the game.

Catcher – Rico Carlo

As any long-time player knows, catcher is where you hide your weakest player. This causes no end of irritation to umpires, who spend their working hours ducking ricochets behind catchers who can't really catch. After realizing that Rico Carlo had neither the arm nor the speed to play right field, Tommy decided that he did have the right tools for catcher: a decent glove, team spirit and a big mouth.

Rico provided an affable cushion between the umpires and our surly pitcher, and also – unlike any other catcher at Double River – actually considered the strategic possibilities of his position. Spotting a chronic pull hitter, for example, he would place his glove on the inside corner, hoping to foul the guy out. At the most, this would create one or two outs per game, but in an offense-minded game like slow-pitch, one or two outs per game makes a difference.

Rico's batting stroke was weaker than Tommy's. No matter where he was actually hitting the ball, Rico appeared to be making an inside-out swing, the bathead lagging behind the handle as if it were made of lead. This created enough variation that he would occasionally get into long streaks (and two .700 seasons). Most of the time, however, he hovered around .400, which was great for Ted Williams but didn't exactly rock Double River.

First Base – Stevie Becker

Stevie made the switch to first after wearing out his legs on a 30-and-over hardball league. Besides, Stevie was a fan of Will Clark, star of the Giants' '89 pennant drive, and wanted to try out some of Will's tricks.

Stevie's main talent was in waiting until the throw left the fielder's hand before deciding which way to pivot. He could effectively flag down anything within five feet of the bag, and saved many an infielder's butt by scooping short-hops. His only flaw was ground balls, which he handled like a true outfielder, swiping at them in the hopes that they might stick to his glove.

Like Will the Thrill, Stevie possessed one of those beautiful, looping left-handed swings, and was constantly pulling nasty-hot drives down the right-field line. This concerned me greatly, as I was often on first at the time. I learned to line up on the foul side of the bag. I later learned that Stevie's up-cut swing was better adapted to hardball, but he cranked it over the right-field fence often enough to be our perennial MVP runner-up.

Stevie was an incredibly positive person with an almost child-like belief in greatness and a deep affection for the history of the game. He was my best friend on the Barons. He was the one who nicknamed me Honus, after Wagner, the great Pirates shortstop, and he loved to tell stories about famous ballplayers from the past.

He held an equal regard for literature – especially great American authors like Hemingway, Steinbeck and Richard Wright – and took great pleasure in having a novelist for a teammate.

A couple other things about Stevie. He exhibited an array of squints, facial tics and throat-clearings that reminded me of the ever-fidgety Jose Canseco (I later discovered this was due to a mild case of Tourette Syndrome). Also, though he seems to be vaguely Hispanic, he is actually half-Irish and half-Chinese.

Second Base – Johnny "Textbook" Silva

The other half of our right side was half-Asian, half-Hispanic, and got his nickname from his shortstop, who admired his grace and consistency. When a ground ball came his way, Johnny would square his feet behind it, bring the glove low and pull it back toward his midsection, then pivot quickly and throw the ball to first. Picture perfect.

It took him a while to figure out his double-play turn. This is difficult, because a second baseman receives the ball with the runner coming at his back. Once he got it, though, he drilled it in and, come game time, did it exactly the same every time: land with his foot on the right-field edge of the bag, hop backward and whip the ball to first.

Johnny and I were a perfect match – no matter what tomfoolery I came up with, he was always ready. We were never close personally, but there were times, on the field, when we seemed to be sharing brain cells.

Johnny's ultimate achievement was playing an entire ten-game schedule without committing an error – this while executing 20 assists and 15 putouts.

Batting-wise, he had a punchy swing that seemed to end about two feet from where it started. He was also a master of the tomahawk chop, fashioning many a hit from pitches that were higher than his head. Though the stiffness of his swing limited his power, it also made him an effective line-drive hitter, and he was usually somewhere between .500 and .600 – a good, consistent range.

Third Base – Gilly McArsten

After the retirement of Alby Thompson, our somersaulting first baseman, Gilly McArsten became our sole African-American – though he was anything but token. When he joined us, he was still trying out for semipro football teams as a wide receiver. He was a superb athlete who possessed an otherworldly control over his body. This and a steel discipline enabled Gilly to become a top-flight player two or three seasons after taking up the sport.

At third base, he fell into occasional slumps – generally when he started thinking too much. But when he was on, forget about it, nothing got by. He was especially adept at line drives, some of which seemed to be past him when he caught them. He was streaky at the plate, too, a tad too stiff and muscular for his own good, but he had impressive power when he needed it, and a good eye for hitting to the center of the field.

His baserunning was sheer ballet. Typically, he would hit a liner into right-center (what earthbound commoners like you and me would call a single), cruise calmly toward first and then, just as the outfielder was picking up the ball, kick it into warp drive. He would achieve second base with a hovercrafting head-first slide that seemed about twenty feet long. I can't recall ever seeing him thrown out, and despite wearing shorts he never got raspberries. It was my theory that he never actually touched the ground.

Gilly also had a lot of fun. He loved competition, and he showed it by talking, whether prodding his teammates, ribbing his opponents, or, when it was called for, talking some smack. I like to think I brought a similar *joie de guerre*, making the left side of the infield the merriest spot on the diamond. And when things got tough on defense, Gilly would crack me up by shouting, "Dig in like an Alabama tick!"

Left Field – Stevie Hammer

Stevie was our first Gen-X'er, bringing youthful exuberance to match his often-spectacular foolishness. We developed a tradition of rookie-abuse on the Barons, but it seems like we beat up on Stevie for five years – until he surprised everybody by taking over as manager during Tommy's hiatus.

I especially remember one spring when Stevie and his housemates ponied up for a soft-core porn channel on their cable. Stevie delighted in giving us weekly updates on his education.

"Oh dude! You shoulda seen this chick last night. She was takin' one guy up the ass and suckin' off another – and she had huge tits!"

Still, I shouldn't knock Stevie too much, because he brought that same wide-eyed enthusiasm to the field. One night I made a diving catch on a liner, and Stevie came running in to give the color commentary.

"Oh dude! You shoulda seen that from left field, man. You were flat-out horizontal and three feet off the ground. Shit!"

I suppose it would have been even more impressive if I had huge tits.

Stevie had excellent speed, and loved to charge in and pick off wannabe singles before they hit the grass. He occasionally paid for this aggressiveness with triples hit over his head, and also suffered from that most common of outfielder maladies, the muffed ground-ball pickup.

At the plate, Stevie lived in a narrow and perilous world – namely, a ten-foot strip extending from the left-field foul line. When his whip-like stroke was properly calibrated, he could land more balls on that stretch of turf than 747s at LAX. Knock the instruments off just a hair, however, and he was nigh-on useless, fouling his way into two-strike counts and then popping up on bad pitches. He occasionally showed an ability to hit up the middle – and with good effect – but seemed to consider it an unmanly compromise.

Left Center – Greg Macy

Stevie's red-headed cohort did everything that Stevie did, but smoother. He made his charging catches, for instance, with a silky-smooth, feet-first slide. His only flaw was the way he held his glove when making catches – stiff-wristed, like a ventriloquist with a dummy.

Talking about Greg's fielding is superfluous, however, because with a bat in his hand he was a goddamned Renoir. His favorite sport was golf, and if you turned the deceptively smooth swing of Tiger Woods horizontal – that was Greg. When we played Double River's notorious field four, with its strong incoming winds, the rest of us adjusted our thoughts to punching ground balls through the infield. Not Greg. He would get up and casually blast a line drive into the teeth of left field, sending it over the fence and halfway up the landfill beyond.

But he was smart, too. Give him two outs and a man on second, and he would turn the golf swing into a tennis forehand, driving the ball over second base for the sure score.

The funniest thing about our outfield was the constant abuse between Greg and Stevie Hammer. Stevie would step into the batter's box and hear Greg shouting, "Hit the goddamn ball! And don't pop out!"

I guess this was their idea of motivation. Occasionally, they would try the same therapy on one of their older teammates, and we would kindly remind them that we had not signed up for the service.

Right Center – Barry Haffinger

My brother-in-law joined the team when I stumbled into one of my sister's coed games. Barry found a spot on the Barons, and I joined up with the WYSIWYGs (high-tech lingo for "what you see is what you get").

Barry's most outstanding feature – especially compared to his fellow outfielders – was his relentless silence. He would go entire seasons without speaking more than two dozen words – and then, quite suddenly, would get a bad call from an umpire and spend the rest of the night riding him from the dugout.

Barry's fielding manner bespoke nothing more than great anxiety. Like Scary Carrie on my company team, he never looked very confident about actually catching the ball, but almost always did. What's more, after he caught it, he could throw it all the way across the complex if he wanted to. His arm strength was such that no one ever wanted to warm up with him. He seemed to arrive at the field pre-lubed, and would nearly tear your glove off with his first throw.

Barry was a "hands" hitter who used a 26-ounce bat to flick line drives across right field (his favorite bat made a "ding" sound like a trolley bell, for which we ribbed him mercilessly). Throw in a footspeed second only to Gilly, and a good eye for balls and strikes, and you had pretty much the perfect leadoff man. When Barry was on, he would hover around the .700 mark. When he was slumping, he had the courtesy to do so for an entire season, making it easier for Tommy to rest him at the bottom of the order.

Barry's arrival (along with a few cameos by my blood-brother, Larry) led to my favorite statistic: the BBI, or brother-batted-in. Since I generally batted directly behind Barry, I couldn't fail but lead the team.

SIX

Shakespeare

In one of my goofier dreams, I envisioned our team in a sixties beach movie where all the guys have hep, archetypal nicknames. The nerdy guy was Poindexter, the short, squirrely guy was Skeeter, and the big dumb guy was Mongo. I would be the suave, intellectual kid, lining up at shortstop with my Buddy Holly spectacles, turtleneck sweater and meerschaum pipe. My nickname would be "Shakespeare."

Alas, my teammates were too literal-minded for this. The only time they were even aware of my other life was when I'd turn down a post-game beer to get to a poetry reading.

Little did they know how the Barons aided my artistic development. I hated feeling rushed before games, so I would show up early and adjourn to the clubhouse balcony. Surrounded by the din of amateur competition, I would practice a form of free association, writing down whatever words came into my head and seeing if they went anywhere.

This ritual contributed to my growing fondness for surrealism, and, not surprisingly, to a couple of softball poems. The first, "Shortstop's Rash," refers to the ant-size scabs you get when you dive across the infield dirt after ground balls. The second, "batbeat," distills a cacophony of softball sounds – pinging bats, scraping cleats – into a critique of modern attitudes: "The game is cloth on dirt / no fred astairing into third but a / decrescendo sled across the gravel." It finishes with a useful warning: "beware the mute outfielder."

Both poems were accepted by journals, which goes to show you – editors know passion when they see it.

I grew so fond of my balcony retreat that I brought the galleys for my first novel there for proofing. When game-time arrived, I handed them to Greg Macy's strawberry-blonde girlfriend, April, for safekeeping.

"Ooh!" she said. "Tell me where all the dirty parts are."

There was a time when I might have taken offense at that, but I had learned my lessons. I began flipping through the pages.

"Well, let's see... Oh, page 87, that's pretty good, and up here around 120 to 123, lots of sex there, and pretty much all of Chapter Twelve..."

By the end of the game, April was hooked. I brought an extra manuscript the following week, and my novel was passed around by my teammates' wives and girlfriends the rest of the summer.

I later promoted a poetry slam with a photo of Gilly's impressive biceps wrapped around a *Norton's Anthology of Poetry*. The photo landed in two local newspapers, drawing a huge crowd to the slam and netting me a promoter's cut of $150 (which translates to about $1,500 in non-poetry money). Gilly was just happy to have celebrity muscles.

The only one of my teammates to display actual artistic talent was my tough-guy manager, Tommy Folgett. When I mentioned I was putting together a small literary journal, Tommy surprised me by offering to do an illustration.

I used to joke that divorce was the number-one cause of bad poetry in America. Tommy was ripe for some of his own artistic therapy. Having survived a long bout with alcoholism, he had been ready for a nice easy cruise, but then Sarnah threw up a brick wall. At the dreaded quarter-century mark (land-mine for young wives everywhere), she started taking night classes and discovered a latent passion for math. She set her sights on a doctorate, and decided there was only one obstacle - the husband had to go.

Tommy was shell-shocked, clutching for straws, and one of them was my journal. I agreed to his offer with some trepidation, then found to my great delight that he was quite talented. Some of his drawings were too slick and cautious, but others carried an appealing dark edge. He was working as a designer at a sign shop, so apparently his artistic leanings were not going entirely untapped. I asked if he would illustrate a poem of mine, and promised to bring a copy to the next game.

I was working as a publicist at an arts center, and had befriended Sandra, a composer of wild, assonant works for exotic groupings of instruments. Her latest was a piece for violin, saxophone, timbales and congas, which she pounded out on her piano one afternoon as I listened, completely entranced. She was having trouble coming up with a title, and asked for my help, asking only that it have some connection to the idea of apocalypse.

We were eating a smoked-salmon pizza in Palo Alto the next day when I jumped off the hood of the car and said, "White Plaid! Get it? If you look at it, it's just white, but because it's plaid there's all these hidden stripes and checks." She loved it.

The piece debuted a year later – Sandra sent me a program – but meanwhile, I was left with a title that demanded a poem. The first part focused on the burst of light from a nuclear explosion, but the final stanza took an unexpected turn.

> The bride wore white plaid
> stealing stripes and checks down the aisle
> The groom's eyes were blue
> and saw only future

After the next game, Tommy followed me to my car so I could give him a copy. As he read it, his face took on an expression of increasing fascination.

"Honus," he said. "This poem is about me."

"Don't be silly," I said. "Your eyes aren't…"

Blame it on male obliviousness, but until Tommy looked up from that poem I had never noticed that he had blue eyes.

Two weeks later, he handed me a pen-and-ink drawing, a breathtaking vision of grace and empathy. A young bride kneels at the foot of a painted pony. She is weeping, having missed her first ride on the carousel.

SEVEN

Bells and Whistles

The Barons team was a self-propelling myth machine. We called ourselves "the legendary Barons" in the hopes that, if we said it long enough, it would come true. Most of our fuel came from Tommy, with his Knute Rockne speeches and on-field bravado. But he also contributed in the areas of statistics and wardrobe.

Every two weeks, Tommy distributed a sheet bearing individual statistics, plus several categorical top-five lists. These included fielding stats (assists, putouts, double plays, fielding percentage), a genre that was shunned by every other team at Double River. At the end of each season, each of us would receive the final stats, make a thorough study of them, and then submit our anonymous ballots for MVP. It was a better-informed, more well-reasoned vote than most Presidential elections.

Tommy's need for numerical precision eventually outgrew the standard scorebook, so he designed his own, adorned with the Barons logo and printed on oversized paper, with its own custom-fit clipboard. The most notable addition was a four-square box at the lower right corner of each batting frame, designed to hold the initials of each baserunner driven home during the at-bat. Although it provided an excellent cross-check for Tommy's late-night compilations, it proved intimidating to the players, only two or three of whom would dare take it on. These duties were eventually taken on by Gilly's long-time girlfriend, Shauna. We were so grateful we named her an official member of the team (the legendary Baroness) and included her in all team photos.

As the stockpile of numbers grew – along with Tommy's need for post-divorce occupation – he began to keep career statistics. He would occasionally announce that one of us had passed some star of yesteryear in career doubles, walks, sacrifice flies – and I must admit, it felt very big-league.

But even this wasn't enough, so Tommy began inventing entirely new statistics. The most durable was RP, or Runs Produced, a figure attained by totaling a player's runs and RBIs and dividing them by his number of at-bats.

Tommy's other triumph was his refutation of the softball maxim, "the nicer the uniforms, the crappier the team." We were often the best-dressed squad at Double River, thanks to Tommy's graphic expertise and traditionalist leanings. He patterned our logo after the Gothic look of his hometown Tigers, and also saved us from two horrid trends in Double River fashion: the purples of the expansion Colorado Rockies and Arizona Diamondbacks, and the great teal invasion brought on by San Jose's first-ever major-league team, the NHL Sharks. There were times during those first few hockey seasons when you could walk into Double River and believe you had just entered an aquarium.

The only real changes for the Barons was from red and navy blue to red and black, and from Detroit Tigers caps to whatever each player had on hand. (Greg Macy wore tennis visors, a sin I will overlook in consideration of his great talent.) We hit our sartorial peak when we went the way of many college teams and adopted a sleeveless jersey – button-up, doubleknit gray with a red-and-white logo – worn with gray pants and an undershirt of red, black or navy blue.

The myth-making expanded as Tommy got into computer graphics. One year he announced spring training with a full-color brochure titled "Barons Throughout History," in which he fused our faces onto old-time baseball photos. Some included witty commentaries. "'Cool Papa' Gilly once flipped the switch and got in bed before the light went out." "Japanese home-run king Stevie 'Saduhara' Becker was known for his high leg kick." He also announced the opening of the Barons website, equipped with player photos, personal news, season schedules and a complete statistical archive.

It wasn't Tommy's slickness so much as how much he cared, how attentive he was to the little rituals that make a legend. One night, I hit for the cycle (single, double, triple, home run), but didn't realize it till after the game. I yelled the news to Tommy as we were stopped at an intersection two blocks from the complex. Tommy immediately scoured the archive and discovered that no Baron had ever done it before (in a game like slow-pitch, this was something of a miracle). Two weeks later, he presented me with the Cycle Award, a plaque of green faux-marble engraved with one of those big-wheeled, turn-of-the-century bicycles. I was genuinely touched.

EIGHT

Barry Bonds, Dodger Blue and the Deaths of Mothers

You don't have much control over the operations of memory, the way your brain goes about attaching certain images to certain events. This is why one of my biggest disappointments reminds me of Barry Bonds, and my greatest tragedy reminds me of the Los Angeles Dodgers.

I got a job at the arts center soon after joining the Barons, and immediately recognized that one day I would see my time there as a kind of golden age. For one thing, I worked in a mansion, bequeathed to the arts center by a U.S. senator. For another, the job of publicity director demanded every one of my abilities: photography, writing, ad design, press relations, and public speaking. I felt fully and joyously employed. I got to meet great performers like Branford Marsalis, Jon Hendricks, Harry Belafonte and Dave Brubeck. I introduced my dad to his boyhood idol, Al Hirt. I was asked to sit next to Harry Connick's lingerie-model girlfriend during his concert. I hung out with the artist residents and picked up little gems of knowledge: the place of repetitions and restatement in compositions (both literary and musical); the perfect touch of Sergei Rachmaninoff on piano; how to get bats to chase pebbles in the twilight.

I like to think it was my influence – limping up the stairs each Monday with my war-wounds – that brought my co-workers to baseball. We interrupted a staff retreat to listen to Will Clark stroke that pennant-winning single in 1989. We spent most of a staff party watching part of that incredible Twins-Braves Series in 1991. And our program director was at Candlestick Park the night of the infamous World Series earthquake (which also brought $500K worth of damage to the mansion).

A couple years later, the Gulf War took a major bite out of our ticket sales, and soon the art center was eyeing its first major deficit. Their first countermeasure was to terminate my position.

In later years, I would sniff out the politics behind my layoff; my duties were transferred to a marketing agency headed by our former box office manager. On the day I got the news, however, I held no bitterness at all. In fact, I ended up having to console my boss, who was pretty torn up about having to tell me. I was ready for something new, anyway, I said. The severance check would give me time to finish my novel. Looking back, I could've handled a couple more years of steady paychecks, but at the time I felt strangely relieved.

With my head full of thoughts, I stuck to my routine that day – shooting hoops at a nearby high school while listening to a baseball game on the radio.

It was playoff time, the Pittsburgh Pirates and a young Barry Bonds, who was already developing a reputation for fizzling out in the post-season. The Pirates were a few innings from elimination when Bonds finally erupted – three-run double, two-run homer, something like that – but at last he had led his team to a playoff victory. I shot three-pointers in the October twilight, thinking how nice it was that I had someone like Barry Bonds to root for.

A few months before (about two years into my Barons career), Stevie Becker invited me to join a hardball league for players over 30. It was great to go back to the "real" game and realize I could still play it. As a "hands" hitter, I avoided the usual perils of switching back from softball, even gained a reputation as a pitcher-killer, wounding four in two seasons with my shots up the middle. I hit .280 my first season, .390 my second, and even got a chance to play in the all-star game at San Jose's minor league field. I played outfield, marveling at how long the fly balls took to come down, and filled in at second and third.

There were some fun moments. I fouled off a former San Diego Padres big-leaguer several times before striking out. I called my own hit-and-run, grounding the ball into right when the second baseman left to cover the bag. I tried a few drag bunts to take advantage of my Kirby Puckett speed ("speed in spite of a belly"). I also got plinked in the head by a curve ball that didn't curve, and failed to turn a double play that would have kept us in the playoffs.

But it was all baseball, and it gave me a new perspective on softball, a sport where you didn't have to contend with 90-foot basepaths, 85-mph fastballs at your chin, and runners with metal cleats. I also noticed that baseball players had more respect for their sport – precisely because it was tougher – and for each other. Suddenly, anyone who got too intense about the pinball machine of slowpitch softball looked pretty goddamn silly.

Another revelation was Stevie Becker, who cranked out homers at a one-per-game ratio, stole bases at a 90 percent success rate, and flashed around centerfield like a demon. I began to wonder why he had never pursued it professionally.

There were, alas, a few negatives. The Sunday doubleheader, a nine-inning/seven-inning combo, was brutal on aging bodies and weekend schedules. Our manager smuggled a couple of 28-year-olds onto the team, a complete violation of the spirit of the league. Third and most tragic, in a league where they wore major-league replica uniforms, Stevie and I played for the Dodgers. For a lifetime Giants fan, it would have been better to play in a hundred-pound suit of armor.

The thing was, though – I needed that team, because my mother was dying. Once her colon cancer metastasized to her liver, I really think she decided to quit fighting it. Mom had gotten a real lemon of a body – chronic hemorrhoids, bad feet, bad back, hysterectomy – and I think she was just fed up with the whole ordeal. My dad gathered us around after her birthday party – just before Memorial Day – and told us she had three months to live.

I will always admire my dad for taking leave from work to look after my mom. But it had an odd side-effect. Beyond a weekly bed-watch, it left us kids with too little to do. So when the games came around – softball on Friday, baseball on Sunday – I suited up and went. I even seemed to play better, because it didn't mean anything. I consoled myself with the knowledge that this is what my mother would want, her son out running in the sunshine, diving on the grass.

On a Sunday in June, I woke up early, took a shower, went through the ritual: pulling on the stirrups, lacing the belt through the pantloops. I was halfway through the door when I spotted the flashing light on my answering machine. It was my dad.

That's how the picture will stay ever after, shafts of morning sun through the sliding glass door, big pine tree off the balcony, Hank Aaron's 44 on my back, a 31-year-old man in Dodger blue, kneeling in front of his telephone, crying.

NINE

From the Inside Out

I began my softball career as a brainless slugger, placed in the third or fourth spot and expected to smack the ball as hard as I could. But the Barons already had sluggers. I eventually settled into the second spot in the lineup, and had to reconsider my approach.

Where a third or fourth hitter is supposed to get runners home, a second hitter is supposed to move them along. It's a subtle shift, but the most effective weapon is clear: hitting to the right.

Right-side hitting has everything to do with the basic geography of the softball diamond. If you hit balls low and to the right, even if you ground out you'll move runners along: second to third, third to home. If you knock it through for a single, your baserunners have a better chance for that extra bag, because the throw from right to third is the longest on the field.

But those are just the obvious advantages. As I honed my new swing, I discovered a world of nuances. My line drives would leave the bat with a rightward spin, causing them to sink after they cleared the infield and take a crazy bounce toward foul ground, leading to many a cheap double. There was also a distinct advantage in hitting toward the weakest fielders on the team.

The rightward approach also provided a solution to perhaps the biggest problem the slowpitch batter faces: an overabundance of options. The high arc of the slow-pitched ball gives the batter too much time to think, and he'll often, for example, go after an outside pitch when his stance is set up for pulling the ball. The body can't take these mixed signals, and 90 percent of the time you'll make an out.

Coming to the plate, I had three strikes to work with and the vision of a perfect pitch: outside corner, belt-high, medium arc. If I got that pitch, I would lower my head to the ball, open up my wrists and follow the stroke smoothly to right field. If I didn't get it, I wouldn't swing. If I ended up with two strikes, I would hit the ball wherever it was pitched.

The effect of my game plan on pitchers was highly amusing. They were likely to pitch the outside corner to begin with, because I was a big guy who looked like a power hitter. Then, if I fouled off the first pitch, they figured they could get me to do it again. So they put it two or three inches further outside, and watched as I smacked it into right field. This often went on all game long, the pitcher working it further and further outside till I was four-for-four and he finally got it into his pea-brain that I could take a ball a foot outside and hit it into right.

The only pitchers who got me were the ones who could hit the inside corner. This took me out of my comfort zone and made me about a .400 hitter. Other times, however, I pulled the switch myself – when I came up with a man on third and less than two outs. Then I would look for something in the heart of the plate and hit it hard, garnering at least a sacrifice fly, possibly extra bases, and once in a while the sight of a ball flying over a fence (sweeter than a naked woman, a hot-fudge sundae or a hundred-dollar bill). This little power-burst also affected the outfield. If they had me pegged as a singles-hitter, I might catch them unaware and send one over their heads. And if that scared them into playing deeper, I had that much more room to land my right-field singles.

The crucial mental aspect of right-side hitting is to stick with the program. You might get overanxious and try to inside-out an inside pitch. You might get robbed by a good second baseman. You might just have a bad day. Never mind. Over the long haul, a batter has to have a system for organizing his thoughts and actions, for focusing. For me, it was hitting from the inside out, and for the most part it was (as they're fond of saying at Double River) money.

TEN

Mirror Game

The most entertaining Barons sideshow was the comings and goings of players and their significant others. Some of these pairings were exceptionally stable, like the Silva family. Johnny's wife and kids would often show up at the games, and we enjoyed the pleasure of watching them grow up over the years. Some of them were surprising. One of our part-time outfielders, Ken, turned out to be the unwed father of my coworker's granddaughter.

The most intriguing, of course, were the rollercoaster rides. Chief among these was the bond between Shauna and Gilly, which, paradoxically, seemed like the most natural relationship in the world. Anyone with doubts about interracial couples should spend some time with these two and pick up the unmistakable aura of soul-mates. It was impossible to picture either one with anybody else.

They were also a physically striking couple. Progressing from his football ambitions to his weight-training business, Gilly maintained his buffed-out physique, and also had an open face and big, friendly eyes that reminded me of another local athlete, football great Jerry Rice. Shauna worked out a lot herself, and her long light-brown ringlets and strong-featured face reminded me of actress Sarah Jessica Parker. Both of them were just nice as hell, and the first couple on anyone's party list.

Eventually, however, the marriage question came up, and Gilly balked. Perhaps he hadn't adjusted his sights from his dreamed-of athletic bachelorhood. Lord knows, he retained the flash and sparkle – like a $50,000 cherry-red jeep, its hood emblazoned with a yard-long black spider.

On the other hand, who the hell knows what goes on inside a relationship? In our disappointment, it was too easy to pull out the "fear of commitment" card. And you had to give Gilly this much: he gave a forthright answer, and now it was up to Shauna to make the decision.

It did put her in quite a spot, though. Bracketed by visions of Gilly on one hand and visions of marriage on the other, she suddenly found that she couldn't have both. She eventually chose a breakup, and though they remained civil, the gameday sight of Gilly and Shauna arriving separately always seemed strange.

Heading the opposite direction was Stevie Becker, hitting his mid-thirties and longing for domestic bliss. I stayed in Stevie's house for a summer, and the first thing I noticed was his unbachelor-like French Colonial furniture. His dating habits, on the other hand, were extremely bachelor-like. His first move toward monogamy was a dating service, which proved to be like throwing gasoline on a fire. Presented with such a smorgasbord of eligible women, Stevie reverted quickly to his rakish tendencies. His morning-after analyses would always begin with the kiss of death, "She's a real sweet lady..."

"You know, Honus, (insert woman's name here) is a real sweet lady, but she just doesn't, you know, float my boat."

Let's just say I was skeptical. If Stevie's boat wasn't being floated, it was sure as hell getting regular trips out of dry-dock.

As for our recovering alcoholic divorcee, Tommy had found the girl of his dreams, at precisely the wrong time. Her name was Lana, a pint-size Filipina distillation of sugar and light. ("And," said Tommy, naming his poison, "another dark, exotic type.") Lana was so open to the world, I found myself giving her a bear hug the second time I saw her.

Problem was, Tommy had dug himself a comfortable foxhole and braced himself for years of surly monasticism. He had even given his manager's trophies to deserving Barons, unable to stand the faux-metal Stonehenge of his lonely apartment. When his dreamboat arrived, so far ahead of schedule, he found himself without the appropriate tickets.

Stevie, meanwhile, had found his own trophy, a sharp redheaded businesswoman who was also hiking the post-divorce minefield. The symbol of her liberation was a backyard koi pond, created by Stevie at the cost of several weekends and many spinal aches. (He recruited half the team to lift a genuine boulder to its shoreline.)

These two tortured romances met on a Friday night at Double River, when Tommy, Stevie and I gathered in the clubhouse for a post-game pizza.

"I am absolutely crazy about Carolyn," said Stevie. "But she's so goddamn jumpy about anything hinting of love, or commitment. I can sit back and say, Yeah, no problem, honey, I understand. You just had your guts ripped out in this terrible, nasty divorce. Hell, just signed the papers last week. But it's so fucking frustrating, so hard to hold back all the things I'd like to tell her. And she works so much, I hardly see her, anyway."

We commiserated for a while, then wandered off on some tangents: how to handle Gilly's injury, what the 'Niners looked like. And then, it was Tommy's turn.

"I just adore the woman, she is so beautiful and sexy, and so good to me. But I wish she would just go away, come back in a year when I'm healed up. After all that shit with Sarnah, I'm just a big pile of Jell-O and scar tissue.

"And then there's work - Jesus! I'm diving into this computer graphics shit, and it never stops. Every time you think you're caught up, some fucker puts out a new piece of software. I haven't got time to be a boyfriend!"

I sat there like Switzerland personified - just listening, as good friends do. But what a testament to male obliviousness, each of them playing the exact role of the other's girlfriend, neither of them noticing. I decided to have some more pizza.

ELEVEN

The I-Told-You-So Tour

The pivotal event of my Barons career occurred three thousand miles east of Double River. But first, I have to tell you about "Silent Night."

It was the only song that Melody Marshall's mother knew, so she used it to sing her daughter to sleep, December or August. Melody asked me and my old choir chum, Anne, to sing it at her mother's funeral. Between the two of us, we knew about a dozen different arrangements, so our final version was pretty exotic. For the last verse, I climbed into a falsetto harmony, and the mourners were left to wonder who was singing what.

Afterward, Anne and I stood on a hill above Cupertino, watching the burial from a non-family distance.

"I guess you heard," I said. "I've invited Melody along on my book tour."

"Yes, I did," said Anne. "And let me just be the first to say, 'I told you so.'"

I knew she was right. Both of us had gone through the rise and fall of our novelty pop band, Serious Cheese, and knew all too well the brand of havoc Melody could wreak. The last straw was the "misplaced" gig fee that ended up in the pocket of Melody's marijuana dealer (she forgot that he was also *our* dealer, which is how we found out).

Was I about to roll flaming briquettes on the patio and do push-ups on them? Probably. But what could I do? My own mother was only two years gone, and Melody had just spent a hellish summer trying to nurse her mom through cancer. And with her small inheritance, at least my cash was safe.

Our third traveler was Billy Giusti, a nerdish but gold-hearted friend who was going to perform various characters from my novel. Billy was a huge Garrison Keillor fan, and quite skilled at dramatic readings. (His best addition to my novel was performing the part of a talking credit card in the voice of Darth Vader.)

We were not yet to the Utah border when Melody pulled me aside at a rest stop and declared that Billy's smarmy personality was driving her up the wall. But no matter – she understood how important this tour was to me, and she would try to hang in there. I could smell the fuse being lit.

The peace lasted for two days. We were clubbing in Kansas City when Melody pointed out a good-looking blonde near the stage and said, "Go talk to her. I've got a feeling about you two."

She was right – the blonde was receptive. We made a lunch date for the next day. When I reported my good news to Melody on the drive home, she realized this would leave her alone with Billy, and conducted a phenomenal about-face.

"I think it's pretty fucking selfish to abandon your friends for some chick."

This lovely little mindfuck ignited my Irish temper, and we found ourselves outside my friend's house in Independence, two in the morning, shouting incongruities at each other until the cops showed up to herd us inside.

That was the end of partying with Melody. When we got to Evanston, Illinois, we handed her the keys to the van (borrowed from Billy's parents) and invited her to let off some steam. She drank all night on the south side of Chicago, returning just in time for me to make my reading in Mishawaka, Indiana. (We stopped in South Bend so she could throw up on the roadside.)

We followed the same routine in Ann Arbor, Michigan. Melody tooled off to the university district, where she slept off her drunkenness in a parking garage (say what you will about Melody, she does not drink and drive).

We crossed into Canada with a bag of pot in Melody's guitar case, taking the land-bridge from Windsor to Buffalo. Whether it was the beauty of Niagara Falls, the startling golds and oranges of a New York autumn, or the exhausting effects of alcohol, Melody began to mellow out. I was greatly relieved, because the main event was about to arrive.

Stevie Becker, the Don Giovanni of first base, had finally met his match. Her name was Tammy Vandermeyer, a charming brunette from Albany, New York. To put it in Stevie's parlance, she wasn't always a sweet lady, but she floated the hell out of his boat.

We got into town just in time for a rehearsal dinner with the Vandermeyers, a stereotypically rambunctious East Coast clan, and Tommy Folgett, who had flown in from California to act as a groomsman. Afterward, Billy and I piled into Tommy Folgett's hotel room, while Melody checked into a lodge down the street for some "alone" time. The boys would need all the sleep we could get, because the next day we were finally (as we had always claimed) headed for the Hall of Fame.

Leaving I-88, heading north for Cooperstown, you begin to suspect that every mid-century illustrator of children's books hailed from New York. When Dick and Jane went to the country, this is exactly what it looked like: trees placed on hilltops like chess pieces, perfect cows with splotches of black and white. And, in every town, that vanilla-white church steeple, looming over everything. Americana illustrated.

I worried that Billy wouldn't enjoy Cooperstown. He was, to say the least, not a sports guy. I probably invited him just so we could leave the van with Melody, who could then blow off more steam tooling around Albany.

Billy wasn't into baseball, but he was definitely into old stuff – and the Hall of Fame was like a century-long antique sale. Most of it was pretty much what I expected, but a few things stand out: a big corner for mah man Hammerin' Hank, and new exhibits on the Negro and women's leagues. I also paid a visit to Honus Wagner in the hall of plaques. My fondest visions, however, were for the tools of the trade: old gloves with fingers the size of hot-dog buns, thick-handled bats that looked like they had been hewn from backyard trees, and ancient, coffee-colored baseballs.

Stevie had affection for the tools of the trade, too, but he had a habit of buying them. His collection included a bat that Ricky Henderson had used in a game, and an autographed group photo of Mays, Mantle and Maris. He spent most of the afternoon prowling the town's memorabilia shops – and he knew he was being a naughty boy, because Tammy had made him swear off such purchases until they had paid for the wedding. Tommy, meanwhile, was displaying all the symptoms of a true believer, staring wide-eyed at exhibits on Tiger greats like Ty Cobb and Al Kaline.

Afterward, we wandered into one of those perfect-looking town squares – lush lawns bracketing cobblestone walks, a big statue of some important-looking dude holding a book. I read the inscription and had one of those "well duh!" moments. It was author James Fenimore Cooper. As in Coopers-town.

Naturally, we had to have a team photo, so the whole squad – Stevie, Tommy, me, Duane (Stevie's hardball coach) and Stevie's other pal Ted – gathered around the revered Mr. Cooper and almost made him smile as Billy pressed the shutter.

The drive back seemed much longer than the drive there. It wasn't five minutes before the inhabitants of Tommy's room were cutting Z's like Musial swatting homers. Morning arrived a little early, however, when Tommy nudged me awake.

"Honus, hey, it's Melody. She's in New York."

"New… huh?"

"New York City."

That got me up. I took a breath and got on the line.

"Mhello?"

"Dude, I am so sorry! I thought, well, we're so close to New York, right? So I might as well check it out, and I found this party in Greenwich Village, and I got kinda drunk so I slept over at some guy's house. But I'll just guzzle some coffee and get back there cause I know you need the van and all. How much time have I got?"

Breathe, Honus. Be calm.

"About two hours."

"Jesus! It's two hundred miles. I better hit the road. I'm so sorry. You're not too mad at me, are you?"

"No, no," I lied. "Just get here as soon as you can. Give me a call when you get in and we'll meet you at the hotel."

"Okay. I'm on it. Bye."

"Bye."

A Manhattan telephone clicked in my ear. I should have been consumed with rage, but instead I felt a lemony, Zen-like peace. I turned to Billy, bleary-eyed in his bed.

"Billy old boy, you and I... have just been liberated."

Here's the thing about me and Melody. As a drummer, I don't have a lot of "chops," but I have a singer's understanding of musical structure and a willingness to be a supporting player. This is what keeps me in gigs. (There's nothing worse than a drummer who insists on wailing away on every song.)

After Serious Cheese, Melody and I formed a guitar-and-percussion act highlighting her songwriting. I geared my playing completely to her whims, because these were her songs. She was the boss. That's how it works.

But my submissiveness gave her a false impression. Honus is such an easygoing guy, and will never tell me no, no matter what I do.

But Melody had never met the Honus who appears when someone fucks with his writing. My reading that day was in Brunswick, Maine, my birthplace, and a town I had not seen in 31 years. By endangering something that precious to me (not to mention the sheer gall of driving the Giustis' van to Manhattan), Melody had just given me license to release the calm pit bull that is the threatened artist.

I smiled neutrally as Melody drove into the lot. I asked about her health as she unloaded her toiletries and guitar. I waited until I had the van keys in my clutches, and then I dropped the hammer.

"Melody, I want you to go home. You're off the tour."

She looked like a five-year-old who's just been told about puppy heaven. She answered through a reservoir of impending tears.

"I know I've been a bitch, Honus, and I'm really sorry, but couldn't you..."

I was ready for this. Melody had a Catholic belief that if you admitted you were a bitch, it was the same as if you actually did something about it.

"Melody, you've been driving us both fucking crazy. I'm sorry, but just get a ticket, make some kind of arrangements – you're not going with us."

The remainder of her defense consisted of unfinished sentences and broken-hearted glances – because she could tell, I had made up my mind. I also had no time, because Billy and I had to hit the road.

Heading northeast out of New York State, we drove in silence, me weighed down by that dreadfully sad look on Melody's face,

Billy afraid that he might be next. But the fall sunshine and the fiery sumac of Massachusetts brought me around, and I turned to Billy and smiled.

"Billy, we're free. The bitch is gone! Yee-hah!"

We made it to Brunswick with just enough light for me to see what a gorgeous place my native town could be, the hard-nosed brick storefronts of downtown, the comforter-thick coating of gold-brown leaves along Bowdoin College. We found the bookstore in a strip mall at the edge of town, and were greeted by employees clearly charmed by my returning-hero status.

Afterward, I stopped in town for gas and coffee, cranking up for the long drive to Albany. But this, like other obstacles to come (the breakdown in Boston, the one-day drive from New York to Atlanta) was pure cake, because the crazy drunken lady was gone. The I-Told-You-So Tour had just come to an end.

The next morning, I drove Melody to the airport. She was flying to Austin, where she and a pal would check out the famed nightclubs of Sixth Street. Standing in line with her was sheer hell, but after she checked in we managed a parting hug and promises to mend our friendship soon (which, somehow, we did). My feelings of guilt were assuaged by the news that Melody had already written a song about me (hey, at least I had provided her with material), but more so by that afternoon's reading in Troy.

There I was honored by the attendance of the bride herself, as well as Greg Macy and his girlfriend April. I also managed to talk Tommy and Stevie into taking parts, typecasting them as softball players "comforting" an injured teammate by recounting gory accidents from the past. Billy, playing the victim, took great delight in letting out pathetic moans whenever his amateur cohorts were struggling to keep a straight face.

After that, it was off to the rental place to pick up my tuxedo and back to the hotel for a rest. I was going to need it, because in a few hours I would catch a prime opportunity to square my accounts with the female gender.

Rosie Konitsky was a beautiful big-boned Polish girl, and one of Tammy's bridesmaids. During a week in which she should have been enjoying her friend's wedding, Rosie had been subjected to the grossly unwanted advances of Stevie's salesman pal, Ted Supern.

Ted was one of those chubby lotharios who does okay at frat parties but can never quite make the adjustment to polite society. Occasionally, this quality comes in handy – such as the bachelor's party, where Ted supplied two young nubiles to perform toy-oriented tricks on each other (I would be lying if I said I was not sorry to miss it). Now, however, it was not handy at all. Ted and Rosie were staying in adjacent rooms at the Vandermeyers' house, and the string of lame flirtations was as steady as an oil leak on an old VW.

"Hey Rosie, you don't have to use that bathrobe when you come out of the shower – cause I'm an open-minded guy."

"I can honestly say that Rosie and I have slept together – at least, under the same roof. Maybe later I'll get to say more."

"Rosie, are you sure you don't need help getting into your dress? I'm very good at… adjusting things."

There's a word for guys like Ted; in fact, there are several. Having so recently stood up for the principles of my art, I was well prepared for my next crusade: getting out the DDT and doing a little dickweeding.

Fate fell immediately on my side. Rosie and I were similar in height, so I was assigned to escort her down the aisle. This pairing remained for the reception, where each couple entered to a public introduction and a round of applause. Being an inch or two shorter than me, dear Ted was introduced directly before us. I noted where he settled at the head table, escorted Rosie to a spot two chairs away, then plopped myself down between them.

The rest was just fucking lovely. Engaging my journalistic interview mode, I spent our dinner peppering Rosie with innuendo-free questions: Where's your family from, Rosie? Oh, did they get out right before the war? So where do you work? What kind of music do you like?

I rigidly avoided the forced connection ("Oh, you like Harry Connick? I met him once."), the flattering comment ("You have the loveliest blue eyes..."), and the sneaky braggadocio – in fact, barely said a word about myself at all. Rosie obviously found all this innocent attention as bracing as an Irish coffee after a day of skiing. I could see her features growing more relaxed, her smiles closer to the surface.

On my right shoulder, I could feel the slow burn of Ted, could almost hear the hissing deflation of his ego. Blocked by my linebacker's body and Rosie's utter engagement, Ted threw in a couple of lame comments and then gave up, spending his time staring into space or making small talk across the table.

Those same blessed pairings applied to the first dance. I stayed with Rosie for three songs, applying my father's lessons in being a good lead. At that point it got tricky, because I was getting rather attached to Rosie myself. If I failed to make a smooth disengagement, if my two hours of graciousness proved to be just another testosterone plea for Rosie's favors, the evening would be irredeemably marred.

When the song ended, I thanked Rosie for her company, begged pardon to congratulate the newlyweds, then returned in another hour, after Rosie had made the rounds of her friends, to dance a couple more. Ted, poor boy, had grown disheartened and gone out to get drunk with a fellow groomsman. The dickweeding was complete, and the grounds were clear for croquet.

The next morning, at the Vandermeyers' breakfast buffet, Tammy pulled me aside.

"Honus, Rosie wanted to thank you for being so sweet to her last night. She said you pretty much saved her whole week."

I must admit, I was thinking about stretching my luck, but when the lovely Ms. Konitsky showed up she looked hung over and worn out. I kept it to a cordial greeting and headed outside for a game of touch football. I returned to find Stevie bragging about my literary achievements (I should have hired him as my agent) and had the sudden urge to hand out free books. Within a half-hour, I had autographed twenty copies, depleting my personal supply and making the Vandermeyers my single greatest concentration of readers.

Once I got back to California, the temptation for a coda finally proved too much, but when Rosie returned my phone message with one of her own and explicitly mentioned her boyfriend (clever girl!), that sealed the deal. Regardless, I will never forget her, because for one day she made me feel like the most gallant man on the planet since Cary Grant in *The Philadelphia Story* or my father on his wedding day.

TWELVE

A Sack Full of Good Intentions

Viewed at night from the bayshore highway, the Double River softball complex was an impressive sight – ten well-groomed fields under a forest of lightstands. The complex offered three automated batting cages, a children's playground and covered volleyball courts, plus a two-story clubhouse with a sports shop, snack shack, arcade and upstairs bar.

The place was founded during the personal computer boom of the early '80s by Joe Mantera, who also ran a performing arts season at a local winery. The winery competed directly with the arts center where I worked, putting me in an interesting position: giving my money to the Manteras every Friday night, and spending the rest of the week trying to take it back out.

Not that the Manteras would have noticed. With headliners like Ray Charles and Roy Orbison, the concert season sold out every year - and Double River was not exactly slacking. On any weeknight, each of its ten fields hosted five league games; the weekends were filled up with tournaments. It was all the groundskeepers could do to keep the players from grinding virtual arroyos into the basepaths. By midsummer, some of them took on the contours of miniature golf courses.

All this success had some nice side-effects. One was the development of a stable, effective umpiring staff. Given a full-time, stationary workplace, the umpires stuck around, developing a rapport with teams and players that cut down on conflicts.

Double River also had a leveling effect on the growing tech/non-tech divide of Silicon Valley. When you passed through that entrance, it didn't matter if you were a semiconductor CEO or a high school janitor. You began to talk as if you came from somewhere like Iowa or Missouri; you drank mass-produced American beers; you scratched yourself and shouted things like, "Ye'm-babe, hup-now, kid! Toss that fire, Big T!"

Shortly after the Gulf War of the early '90s, the Manteras suffered some sort of financial setback - as I recall, an unexpected callback on a sizable loan – and decided to take it out on their most reliable cash cows, the softball players of Silicon Valley.

The first warning shot was the Great Token Deflation. Double River charged a one-dollar admission fee, in exchange for a one-dollar token that could be used at the batting cage, bar or snack bar. We arrived on opening day to find that the exchange rate value had been reduced to fifty cents – a minor but symbolically significant change.

Then came the Missing Umpire Conspiracy. Games that had always been called by a base umpire and a plate umpire were now called by the plate umpire alone (he was also responsible for recording outs and runs on the electronic scoreboards). This came with the news that players would begin their at-bats with one-and-one counts. You could say that this was done to take some pressure off that one lonely, multi-tasking ump. I figured it was done in order to herd the cash cows in and out more efficiently.

Finally, there came the Facilities Maintenance Crisis. The light standards had so many missing bulbs that grounders seemed to come out of dark caves. The same affliction struck the scoreboards, creating numerals that resembled Greek letters ("I'm not sure, but I think we're winning Alpha Gamma to Delta Upsilon"). In the batting cage, the pitching machines became as unhittable as Pedro Martinez, and we had numerous opportunities to practice our high-school Spanish on the workers: "Ayudame, por favor! Machina numero seis!"

The Mantera properties were soon put under bankruptcy protection, and I placed my fondest hopes in the rumor that Double River would be purchased by the City of Sunnyvale. My hometown had a well-deserved reputation for doing things right, and I certainly trusted them more than the Manteras, who had a long record of indictments-but-no-convictions in the world of real estate development.

Alas, Sunnyvale dropped out, and the Manteras signed some sort of protection arrangement – complete with another hassle for the players. The Manteras had been disallowed from contracting directly with the umpires' union, so now each team had to go to the umpire before each game and fork over nine bucks cash.

A few months later, my former boss at the arts center hooked me up with an independent publisher who had agreed to produce a program magazine for the Manteras' winery concert season. After coordinating several such magazines at the arts center, I was perfect for the job, and grateful for the work. About a week after the project was completed, I stopped by the office to pick up my check and heard an interesting story from my publisher, Jack.

Cognizant of the Manteras' habit of not paying their contractors (because they had no money to pay them with), Jack rode shotgun on the delivery truck. When they arrived at the winery, he declared that not one copy of his magazine would exit the back of that truck until he was holding a full cash payment in his grubby little publisher's paws.

Appalled at this grotesque lack of trust, Joe Mantera drove Jack to the Double River complex, where he scoured out every single cash register – admissions gate, snack bar, nightclub, league office – and handed his pickings to my publisher in a brown paper sack.

I was grateful for my on-time paycheck (a rarity in freelance writing), but I could see the dark clouds shadowing our happy hunting ground. This here cash cow was about to be milked for all it was worth, and the Barons and their rivals were all on board for a joyless toboggan ride to the bottom.

THIRTEEN

A Prayer and a Crotch

My personal façade was developing some cracks as well, troubling signals that my faith in our self-created myth was wavering.

The first involved Gilly's fondness for leading team prayers before playoff games. For years, I would cope with these little comedies the same way I handled prayers at church weddings – just bow your head, think positive thoughts, and when somebody says "Amen," it's back to business. Since Gilly's petitions were well-chosen ("keep us from harm, let us play our best"), this was not too difficult.

As the years passed, however, my feelings began to shift. I had become an active agnostic, and, regardless, thought it demeaning to drag anybody's god into something so trivial as a sporting event. The next time Gilly gathered the troops and took a knee, I slipped off toward the bleachers, hoping nobody would notice.

"Hey Honus," said Stevie Hammer. "Where ya goin'?"

So much for anonymity. I waved a hand and said, "It's all right, go ahead," then pretended to tie my shoelaces.

Afterward, I found Gilly walking my way. I wasn't sure what to tell him. I think I came up with something like, "I'm sorry, it just doesn't fit in with my beliefs."

"Hey, that's fine," said Gilly. "I totally understand. I wouldn't want you to do anything you're not comfortable with. Now let's go play some softball, okay?"

Wow, I thought. *That was much too easy.* But it did leave a mark, because it was the first time I put my own beliefs ahead of team unity.

The second occasion came during a game with my coed team, the WYSIWYGs. Although Double River had not yet cut the second umpire, the inconsistency of their paychecks had driven out many of the veterans. This meant we were sometimes stuck with pimply-faced rookies with little knowledge of how to call a game.

The kid we were breaking in that night looked like he hadn't started shaving yet. His strike zone was moving around like a kite in heavy wind, and I spent the first few innings giving him an earful from short.

But first, a little background. If a major league shortstop questioned balls and strikes from the field, he would likely get himself thrown out of the game. At Double River, if you ejected a player and his team didn't have a ready replacement (which was often the case), the game was forfeited. This had the opposite of the intended effect. Because an ejection carried such a heavy penalty, the umpires were reluctant to throw anybody out. Recognizing this reluctance, the players figured they could get away with anything.

Another important piece of information. Like most players, I had developed a series of pre-pitch rituals. I would sweep the ground in front of me with my cleats (a habit I picked up from A's third baseman Carney Lansford), then settle into my crouch with three distinct movements. I would plant my right foot, then my left, and then I would reach across with my throwing hand, pinch a piece of fabric on my left thigh, and hitch up my pants.

By the fifth inning, I had tired of ragging on the kid umpire – and even sorta wondered why he hadn't given me a warning yet. He still hadn't nailed down his strike zone, however, so when our opponents were awarded yet another dubious walk, I let out a loud sigh, shook my head in disbelief and went into my ritual. When I reached over to hitch up my pants, the kid umpire thought I was giving him the old Brooklyn crotch-grab. He immediately jumped from behind the plate and announced that the shortstop had just been thrown out of the game.

The manager and I descended on home plate, pummeling the kid with protests. I explained my ritual pants-hitch, and said that, at least, he should have given me a warning first. A senior umpire wandered by to investigate. He agreed with us about the warning,

THE LEGENDARY BARONS · Michael J. Vaughn

but, in typical Double River fashion, was unwilling to do anything about it.

In the meantime, who should show up but Tommy Folgett. Tommy was going through a trial separation with Lana, who had gone to Hawaii to reclaim her kids from her grandparents. Tommy had developed a crush on Judy, our redheaded first basewoman – a ferociously insecure bitch from Colorado who could've chewed him up in a New York minute. Such was his motive for showing up early to catch our game.

We were lucky enough to have a replacement player, but without a real shortstop (our first-stringer, Mitch, was injured), we suffered a solid whupping. After the final out, Tommy strolled over for a talk with the kid umpire.

"You know what happened?" he started. "You let your ego get in the way of doing your job. You got a problem with the shortstop? Guy's mouthin' off too much? Fine. You call time, you say, Sir, you will refrain from complaining about balls and strikes or I will throw you out of this ballgame. Guess what? You have just taken the problem from your shoulders and placed it on his. He says anything after that, that's his choice, and Wham! He's out.

"The way you did it was a total set-up. You stand there like a statue for five innings, taking in all that abuse, then the guy scratches himself and blammo! Suddenly you, and not the players

deadendstreet.com   68 on the field, have decided the game. You blew it. And I'll tell you what. You better get used to a lot of action in the crotch area, because we wear these protective devices called cups, and once in a while you just gotta reach down there and make some adjustments."

It was an absurd evening all around – the first ejection of my life, caused by an optical illusion. But it was a helluva lot of fun watching Tommy Folgett work over that umpire. He was like the long-lost illegitimate son of Billy Martin, and I was grateful that he would give me such a sparkling defense.

The phantom crotch-grab resulted in years of ribbing from my coed teammates (who considered me too intense to begin with). But I did have my redemption.

A month later, I was playing a tournament with the Barons when the base umpire came out between innings to greet me.

"You're right. You make that move every time."

"Huh?"

"That way you hitch your pants. I've been watching you, and you do it before every pitch."

I still wasn't quite getting it, so he filled in the blanks.

"That night you got ejected. I was the base umpire."

"Oh, it's you!" I said. "Boy, that's funny."

At Double River, you never knew when and in what guise your deliverance might come. It might even come from an umpire.

FOURTEEN

Mitch, Willie and the Duke

Tommy had a sprained ankle one week and told us that Willie Sandrejas would be filling in at pitcher. Sort of like saying that Robert DeNiro will be filling in at your high school play.

It wasn't that Willie's pitching was all that exceptional – a no-fuss wrist-flick that came in on a low arc – but his fielding... It was like someone had constructed a brick wall extending three feet to either side of the rubber. Nothing was getting through, and Willie assumed a number of yoga positions to get a glove (a foot, a knee, his right ear) on the ball.

With the disappearing-ball act in front of me, my dashes toward second base turned into one soft-shoe after another. And with a man on first and two out, Willie covered second base, allowing Johnny Silva and I to play deep.

On offense, Willie had reduced the hitting of a softball to a precise and limited science. If the pitch verged to the outside, he would hit a line drive that landed not more than three feet fair down the right-field line. Inside pitch – same thing, left-field line. It was like his wrists were built on a two-way hinge. Even when the defense figured him out and played him literally on the foul lines, odds were, at the end of the play, Willie would be standing on second, exchanging recipes with your shortstop.

It was even more fun on those occasions when Willie had to settle for a single. He would round first at full speed then lock up the brakes, sliding along on his cleats like miniature skis.

I found out that Willie was something of a legend, that he would show up every night to play four or five games, with different teams and in different positions. Despite his talent, he had not one ounce of ego. He seemed to know every man, woman and child who walked into Double River, and greeted me by name every time he saw me, even though he must have played with 327 different shortstops. He should've run for Congress.

As the years passed, I developed a long list of questions for Willie. How did he manage it? Understanding wife? Graveyard shift? Lottery winner? But I never asked him. Why ruin a legend with petty facts?

So let me tell you about the catch. It's summertime, and Stevie Hammer has booked us into a tournament in Santa Cruz. We're playing at a tiny field with high fences, necessitating a home-run limit of six per game. We suffer a quick loss, and face the dreaded "lose two and barbeque." Second game, we're hanging on to a one-run lead going into our opponents' last at-bat, but they've got runners on second and third with two out. The next batter nails a drive toward the left-center gap. The infield holds its collective breath.

Before the ball can reach the fence, however, an object resembling Willie streaks in from center. The thing about what happens next is not so much the act itself as the premeditation. Willie strikes the ground with both feet, like Louganis off the five-meter board, and then takes flight. Freeze him in place – snap! – and he is four feet above the ground, completely horizontal, his back parallel to the fence two feet behind him. The ball pops neatly into his glove, he manages to land without separating a shoulder, and his teammates turn into drunken cowboys.

We lose the next game and head home. Nobody cares. We have seen something joyous.

Our next hero is Mitch Kashahara, the shortstop for my coed team. It was Mitch's sheer talent that returned me to the Willie Mays outfield fantasies of my youth. Guy hits a drive, you turn your back to the infield and sprint, turn at the track to find the ball coming in over your right shoulder, smack! into your outstretched glove. (The runner, who didn't bother to tag up at third, returns sheepishly to his base as his teammates rag him mercilessly.)

At shortstop, Mitch had a wider range than a Texas cattleman. He could dive as far and as smooth as Willie, plus he was a foot taller. He didn't throw very hard, but he had a quick release that seemed like an optical illusion – like he threw the ball before he actually caught it.

At the plate, Mitch was a pitcher's worst nightmare. He would lunge forward, get his hands way out front and use a mighty wrist-flick to send cup-seeking missiles back through the box. One season, I encouraged him to hit for the fences, but it didn't work – he was too dialed-in for line drives. He hit a homer once, but it never got more than ten feet off the ground. We're still not sure if it went over the fence or through.

Mitch's only flaw was his conviction that he should be able to field any ball within the sound of his voice. One time he broke early on a pull hitter and dove on a ball in the outfield grass – after it had gone through the third baseman's legs. But he was pissed, because he couldn't make the throw to second. After the third out, he slammed his glove to the bench and said, "Dammit! I should have had that one."

Shortstop is tough enough without self-flagellation, so I offered some brotherly condolence.

"Mitch, the guy in the comic books with the telescoping arms couldn't have made that play."

I soon realized that such offerings were lost on Mitch. He was a little too fond of beating himself up. So I joined him.

"Yeah, yaknow, Mitch, I spend my weekends telling everybody what a sucky shortstop you are. My three-year-old niece could've made that play, and frankly she throws like a girl."

I'm not sure if that helped. But it sure was fun.

I also came to realize that, when it came to shortstop, Mitch and I were dead even. The great equalizer was hubris. Like an attentive lap dog, I studied each passing mood of the softball gods and adjusted my ambitions accordingly. If my second baseman made a bad feed, I gave up on the double play and made sure of the force at second. If I caught the ball too deep in the hole for a throw to first, I was content to hold the runner at third.

Mitch, on the other hand, was an infield Icarus, catching his wings on fire, trying impossible throws that inevitably ended up in the outfield or down the foul line. In other words, Mitch made more plays than me, but he also fucked up more plays.

It was that very risk-taking mentality, however, that would later win my eternal admiration. Mitch worked for years as the graphics guy in a high-tech marketing department. It was boring work, but highly paid, and it supported a long list of outdoor activities.

Unlike so many who talk of longing for an artistic life, Mitch actually did something about it. He took an entry-level position at a computer animation firm – at half his previous salary. A few months later, we were stretching out before a game, and I asked him about the new job. His face lit up.

"You know what we did today, Honus? We had a two-hour meeting about animating Daffy Duck's spit!"

We were thrilled, a couple years later, to see a Spielberg film with the voices of Sharon Stone and Woody Allen, and see Mitch's name in the credits. Minor celebrity seemed an odd match for such an unassuming, mild-mannered soul – but he wasn't done yet.

Mitch had never had much luck with women. He had suffered the same attraction for our redheaded first basewoman that later afflicted Tommy. When his feelings went profoundly unanswered, Mitch settled for a friendship that made two things pretty obvious: Mitch would never entirely give up the attraction, and Judy would make him pay for it whenever possible.

Mitch finally found closure when Judy found Max – surely the most understanding man on the planet. A while later, Mitch met Dawna, a charming, soft-spoken divorcee with two young daughters.

But there was more. I got the word from Lisa, our resident rocket scientist (no really, she worked for NASA).

"Did you hear about Mitch's new girlfriend? She's Duke Snider's daughter."

I was instantly jealous. During the great New York rivalries of the '50s, Duke was on the same level as Willie Mays and

Mickey Mantle, but without their household-name publicity. This gave him a certain mystique. Even the place where he gained his fame, Ebbets Field, was gone, a phantom. The name "Duke Snider" carried a certain element of myth – but here he was, still young enough to have a daughter who was dating my shortstop.

When we were introduced, I tried so hard not to make a big deal out of it that I made a big deal out of it. Even as the months passed and Dawna became less daughter-of-Duke, more the nice lady who played third, I continued to eat up her celebrity childhood stories.

I assumed that she was probably tired of hearing about her dad. Actually, she loved nothing better than talking about him – and why wouldn't she? One day she brought a limited-edition Duke Snider glove, a gift from her dad, and used it in a game. Again, why wouldn't she?

I was surprised to learn that Dawna, approaching her 40th birthday, had never played a sport involving bats and balls. In fact, the slugger gene was nowhere to be found. And she wasn't much of a fielder. But once in a while, a little streak of Duke would show itself. One night, she went five feet up the line to fetch a bad throw, with a runner coming into the bag. Suddenly, mild-mannered Dawna Snider was hurling herself headlong at the runner, whapping her across the forehead. The runner complained bitterly (coed females being much prissier than their women's-league counterparts), but her ass was out.

I took to using my new connection as a kind of litmus test. When I mentioned that I played softball with Duke Snider's daughter, I got two distinct reactions. One was the blank look and "Duke... who?" – for which they were exiled to a mild (but permanent) purgatory. The other was a wide-eyed look, followed by "Really? Duke Snider?" For which they were awarded early admission to my inner circle of friends.

My fondest hope was that Papa Snider would come to watch his daughter play, be impressed by the outfielder with the deceptive Kirby Puckett speed, and offer to autograph his glove. He showed up twice – and both times, I was away on vacation. After the first of these, I asked Mitch if he had been nervous, playing in front of his potential Hall-of-Fame father-in-law.

"Are you kidding me?" he asked. "I sucked!"

FIFTEEN

The Assholes Appeareth

The neglect brought on by the Manteras' bankruptcy, the disappearance of half the umpires, and the coming-of-age of a generation weaned on No Fear athletic goods combined to produce a new breed of sports asshole.

The first wave arrived along racial lines. The young Latino teams drew on the fine cultural tradition of machismo, employing a wide array of bush-league tricks: calling "out of play!" when their batters hit perfectly catchable foul pops; yelling "down!" from the coach's box to make you think there was a runner coming to your base. If you complained about any of this, their first line of defense was to threaten to kick your ass. Charming.

The other race war had a name: Superfly. In the years of Rodney King and O.J., in the world's capital of political correctness, the all-black Superfly team figured they could get away with anything. The weapon of choice was trash-talking, and the white boys were pretty screwed no matter how they responded. Talking back didn't work because 1) we were no good at it, 2) it tweaked our feelings of white guilt, and 3) if we really got pissed off, they would laugh at us, 'cause hey, it's just talkin' smack, man (these white boys are so sensitive!). Our only lines of defense were Gilly (our cultural translator), and running up the score – which seemed to be the only way to shut them up.

Every game with Superfly was a test of mental survival, and the worst among them was Rollo Simkins. Rollo was a gelatinous young man who was actually quite a good pitcher, equipped with an array of quick-pitches, junk pitches, differing arcs and angles. Plus he had a number of dekes and fakes to throw you off your rhythm. But just getting you out wasn't enough for Rollo – he had to make you suffer. His favorite trick was to field a grounder and then roll it to first for the putout (in the majors, Rollo's next plate appearance would begin with a fastball to the head).

You could usually fend off Rollo's quick-pitches by calling time-out until you got settled in the box. One night, the umpire, a black man, decided he would not be granting time-outs, so I stood outside the box, staring down Rollo's ugly puss until he might decide to step off the mound for a second. No dice. He stood there, arm at the ready, and said, "Get your fat ass in there."

This might have struck me as funny – Rollo's own derriere being the size of Kentucky – but too many games against Superfly had deprived me of my sense of humor. For a split second, I got a glimpse of the homicidal impulse, could envision taking this aluminum bat in my hands and smashing in that goofy melon of his. No one should have to face down their darkest impulses while playing something so trivial as a softball game. So I got my fat ass in there.

The most powerful conglomeration of assholes at Double River was not Superfly, however, but a miniature political elite I will call The Tribe. These were the folks who had no lives outside softball, who hung out at Double River every night, ate pizza before the game, partied in the bar afterward, and developed a tightly knit circle.

Fanatic devotion to a sport is no sin, but the members of the Tribe weren't happy just playing softball with their friends. What they wanted was guaranteed fun, and fun to them meant winning. Their favorite strategy was to sign up for leagues far beneath their level and spend their weeknights whomping relative beginners.

This meant that no one else had a chance to win a championship. Complaining was useless, because the management was not about to crack down on their best paying customers.

This nasty trend didn't affect the Barons – we played in the upper leagues, anyway – but it showed up on a regular basis in the coed leagues. For a number of years, playing on the WYSIWYGs was like being an enslaved Jew in Egypt – and the Pharaoh was a team called Triple Crown. The brand of softball they played was so spiritless and lazy (owing to a lack of challenges) that we could occasionally sneak up and beat them. But even this was a cruel hoax. Come the playoffs, their A roster would reappear to smite all comers.

Just to add to the torment, one of Triple Crown's regulars was my stepbrother, Jerry, a talented player who lollygagged his way through games in a pair of plaid picnic-style shorts. I found out later that my stepmother was making a quilt out of Jerry's many championship T-shirts.

Triple Crown's pitcher, Daniel, had only one arm. He addressed this obstacle in the same way as the majors' one-armed Jim Abbot, tucking his fielding glove under his nub and then shifting it to his hand after releasing the pitch. With his one-armed swing, he had less control, but didn't lack power – he occasionally hit balls over the fence.

This would have been more inspiring were it not for the fact that Daniel was a surly, overcompetitive jerk. One night I put a hard slide on his girlfriend, a six-foot-two athlete who regularly hit balls out of the park herself. After the play, Daniel turned around to cuss me out, mentioning something about his girlfriend's recent ankle injury. I shouted back that 1) I didn't get the scouting report on the ankle, 2) if she's going to play shortstop, she should learn to get the hell out of the way of sliding baserunners, and 3) I was damned if they were going to turn a double play when my team was losing by 15 runs. Fortunately, our shouting match was kept to shouting, while the fragile six-foot-two shortstop shed a few demonstrative tears.

The ultimate case of bad sportsmanship came from another shortstop-pitcher duo, this on a squad called the A-Team. I stepped to the plate in the sixth inning with two on and two out, and my team down by 12 runs. I figured if I could hit one out, we could take the lead down to nine and at least avoid the ten-run "mercy" rule. The pitcher, a hefty blonde, was thinking the same thing. Spotting the weak-hitting Judy on deck, she threw two low, fast pitches a foot outside. When I found a third headed for the same spot, I lunged out and knocked a double down the line.

If we had been in a close game, I wouldn't have bitched about it. But I was just looking to save my team some dignity – so I bitched about it plenty.

"What kind of chickenshit maneuver was that?" I shouted from second. "You in a hurry to get somewhere? Can't even give me a fuckin' chance?"

"What the hell do you want?" replied the pitcher. "You got a double, didn't you?"

"That's not the point and you know it, goddammit."

At that point, the shortstop, a six-foot-three bodybuilder type, came valiantly to his pitcher's defense.

"Hey! You don't talk to my pitcher like that. She's a lady, all right?"

"No lady pitches like that," I said.

"I'll kick your fuckin' ass right now, pal."

Well, there you go. My evening was complete. My team was getting its aggregate butt whipped by a team that should have been playing two levels higher, I had just been screwed out of a chance to hit a face-saving homer, and now Jesse Ventura's little brother was threatening to kick my ass. What a lovely place to play softball.

I wisely (but not easily) swallowed my pride and just stared at the guy like I didn't *hablo Ingles*. Judy grounded out weakly to third, and the A-Team was righteously appalled when I didn't come out to shake their hands and thank them for a "good game."

Assholishness is difficult to defuse. I can think of only twice when I came anywhere close. Once was when this 19-year-old Latino kid slid into second base ahead of my tag and let out some video-game slogan like, "Not even close – nevah gonna get me!" I patted him on the head and said, "You're so cute when you're sassy!" Which both confused him and, I think, scared him a little.

The other was one of those situations where I was complaining to the umpire over a call, and the runner – who should've been reveling in the fact that he'd been called safe – chipped in with some witty observation like, "Fuck you, asshole!" Judging his IQ at the possum level, I initiated a game-long campaign of nonsense vocabulary.

"You are detestably pusillanimous."

"Your mother cavorts with disestablishmentarianist zygotes."

After a couple innings, he stopped listening – which was fine with me.

Thoughts of Double River began to depress me. Especially when the management responded to the tensions they themselves had created by instituting a one-out penalty for use of the f-word. I considered calling the ACLU and initiating a free-speech protest.

I recall Tommy's advice regarding Superfly: "The only way to shut them up is to beat them." But why should that be so? Why should I expend so much energy staying clear of assholes (and, what was harder, trying not to become one myself)?

I envisioned a place where I could play my beloved game and enjoy myself, win or lose, oh-for-three or five-for-five. I had a feeling it wasn't going to be at Double River, and that was bound to bring a dilemma.

SIXTEEN

Time Out

Then, quite suddenly, I was relieved of duty. After a disastrous venture into a higher league, Tommy announced that he was calling it quits. The combination of career demands, his dying relationship with Lana, and the lobbying of the younger players who wanted to stay in the higher leagues, had finally worn him out. Stevie Hammer talked of taking Tommy's duties – as he had during Tommy's post-divorce sabbatical. But then Stevie Becker bowed out, citing the fertility program he was going through with Tammy. That was enough for me. I threw in the towel, happy to be rid of Double River (the WYSIWYGs had also dissolved, thanks to a final rift between Judy and Mitch).

Like any long-time junkie, I had my backup stash. I had been playing in a men's league in Sunnyvale. They had two umpires and a scorekeeper, plus players who actually seemed to be there to have fun. Imagine that.

I also enjoyed some major advantages, principal of which was a return to the standard zero-and-zero count. Given an extra strike to work with, I smoked enough grounders through that right-side gap to wear out a small trench. In my first season, I hit a rather incredible .850, and earned the nickname "Automatic." I also got a chance to play some more outfield, offering welcome rest to my thirtysomething knees and overtaxed brains (say what you will about smart outfielders through history, it's still a _ob that could basically be performed by a labrador).

Still and all, it was nice to get a call from Tommy four months later, asking if I'd like to play on his company team. The games were at Double River, but the company leagues were notoriously relaxed, so I was pretty sure the asshole factor would be kept to a minimum.

Playing behind Tommy again felt downright nostalgic, not from any great passage of time, but because I had assumed I might never play with him again. It also highlighted our psychic advantages. After one eager-beaver pulled two pitches foul, I knew Tommy's next pitch would be about two inches inside and a little high, that the batter would be forced to put it in play, and that his weak, short-armed swing would produce a chopper between me and the third baseman. I broke with the pitch and was waiting when the ball arrived.

After the game, I bummed a cigarette from Tommy (which I immediately ordained as my new post-game ritual), and Tommy asked if I wanted to go somewhere for a chat. We headed for a coffeehouse in Campbell with blondewood furniture and a warehouse ceiling, and settled at a table outside so Tommy could smoke. I was surprised to see that he had purchased a beer.

"Yeah, that's one of the things I wanted to tell you about. There's something sorta all-pervasive about A.A., yaknow? I went seven years – seven years! – without so much as a drop, and I think I'm ready to try a little moderation."

Item number two was Lana. She had returned from Hawaii, having failed to win back her kids, and things between them had fallen apart. I had to guess a lot of the details, but it sounded like Lana had come back under a cloud of pointlessness, had gone a long time without finding a job, and become more and more dependent on Tommy. Tommy asked her to move out, even got her an apartment and paid the first few months' rent. Now, he was ready for the next step.

"If I was anywhere else, with my skills, I'd be making a lot more money. But to the sign company, I'll always be the kid without the college degree who's been there forever. So I'm starting my own business. I've got a couple projects lined up already. It's gonna be a hellacious amount of work, but ya know? I got no girlfriend and no Barons, so there's no time like the present.

"But I do have a little issue with cash flow, so I was hoping you might be able to help me out, Honus. I've got an extra bedroom in my house, and an extra bathroom. I'd like to rent them to you, for four hundred dollars."

Since my cross-country writing tour the year before, I had been sleeping on the living room floor of Anne, immortal titler of the I-Told-You-So Tour. Although the arrangement brought a delightfully low rent to the both of us, Anne was growing weary of stepping around my head each morning. Tommy's offer seemed like the perfect solution.

In the middle of our conversation, I sensed something dark and slippery passing over my feet, and turned to find a labrador pup in Tommy's lap, threatening to lick his face off.

"Well!" said Tommy. "Where did you come from, fella?"

A young yuppie-looking guy walked up in jogging clothes, apparently on a search mission.

"Oh," said Tommy. "Does he belong to you? He's a cute one."

"Actually," said the man, "he just showed up in my front yard this morning – no tags or anything. I've been trying to figure out what to do with him. You want him?" The pooch sat down on Tommy's shoetops and delivered his most adorable expression, a tongue-lolling grin straight off a pet-store calendar.

"Ya know," said Tommy. "Strangely enough, I think I do."

Ten minutes later, I walked Tommy and his new friend back to his Camaro. Tommy took a look at his perfect sky-blue interior and instructed the labrador to please contain all bodily fluids until they got home. I agreed to help Tommy at his garage sale that Saturday, at which time I could also check out the room.

Tommy gave his back seat a worried look and said, "I don't know, Honus. Do I know what I'm doin' here?"

"None of us do. He is awfully cute, though."

I showed up Saturday to find the labrador gone. Tommy had deemed himself unfit for puppy-raising, and had given him to a friend with a wife, two kids and a big backyard. But it was clear that the dog was only the first of many things Tommy was looking to be rid of. He had enough furniture in his driveway to fill a good-sized apartment, and was taking the tiniest of offers: thirty bucks for an entertainment center, twenty for a coffee table. A wonderful old drafting table went for thirty-five.

"It's amazing, Honus. A house is just a big ol' stuff-magnet. You just keep collecting furniture, then you wake up one day and you haven't got room to cut a fart."

After we cleared out the big-ticket items, I went inside to check out the room: big crack in the window, a view of the neighbor's fence, but what did I care? It would be my very own personal space.

Of course, by then I had been softened up by Tommy's neighborhood. It was one of those brilliant October mornings that always reminded me of '49ers games at Candlestick Park, sunlight slicing through the streets like the Earth had just shed an extra layer of atmosphere. The deciduous trees were launching an all-out attack – sycamore, maple, birch and liquidambar – enough to remind me of my last two autumns in New York.

After dragging in the last unsold items, Tommy and I shook hands on the new arrangement, and I said I would move in the following weekend. But I wish he had kept that labrador.

SEVENTEEN

Trashing the Trophies

My low rent got even lower when Tommy swapped a couple months' payments for some painting. I slept in the guest bedroom while I covered my bedroom-to-be in bone white, then continued to the living room. After that, I did Tommy's bed and bath in doeskin, a light brown with a touch of butterscotch.

Tommy seemed to enjoy the new brightness, which added further to the feeling of space created by his cleared-out furniture. Our feelings of camaraderie were also furthered by the company team. As wise old veterans surrounded by novices, we quickly took to our positions as teachers. We kept our patience when someone forgot to cover a bag or dropped an easy fly – and exulted when one of our "hard cases" beat out an infield hit or made a nice throw. Tommy was also enjoying his new role as a hitting star – and driving the ball much farther than he did as a Duke.

The team took the championship pretty handily. On the night of our playoff doubleheader, the softball gods seemed happy to grant me whatever I wanted. I remember one play in great detail. Some guy blooped a ball over my head, and I ran straight back, knowing that my corporate outfielders would be playing deep. But

I ran too far, and turned to find the ball descending to my left. I hit the brakes with a double-wing slide, legs folded out on either side, and reached far to my left to pocket the ball.

More than the victories, however, Tommy and I were enjoying the lack of pressure, the rediscovery of softball as just a game. We had officially begun our post-Barons period, and we soon found a way to mark the passage.

Tommy still had several championship trophies gathered around his fireplace like a band of tiny brass gypsies. One morning we loaded them into a truck, along with some junk from Tommy's sign business, and headed for the landfill. After backing up to our spot and throwing away everything else, we took turns tossing out our victories, dedicating each to some lesser-known Barons player.

"This one's for Grant!" said Tommy. Summer 1995 struck a pile of bricks, spitting out plastic parts.

"And this one," I said, "is for Franz!" Fall 1996 landed in the mud with a sploosh!

Tommy treated me to lunch, then we headed home and left our muddied-up shoes in the garage. Tommy's looked pretty new, but he never wore them again.

There was a good side to Tommy's fussiness. One time, I asked him to whip up a flyer for a poetry reading. After a half-hour, he handed me an art-deco blend of stylized lettering and ravishing ornaments worthy of a 1930s MGM film poster. He apologized for the "roughness" of the work. He was also working on a Barons memorial web site, and over the course of several weeks you could pass by his office and find him staring at the same home-page logo, adjusting imperfections far beyond the average person's grasp.

His great affection for the Art Deco movement of the early 20th century graced the living-room walls, in the form of several tastefully framed prints. When he discovered a seventysomething illustrator of roadsigns from this period, Tommy ordered up all his books and offered to help him set up signings on the West Coast.

Another of Tommy's enthusiasms was for women's figure skating. You could attribute some of this to the finely shaped derrieres of its practitioners, and the scanty outfits that showed off same, but that didn't explain everything. During the Winter Olympics in Nagano, Japan, I would arrive home to find my tough-as-nails manager glued to the set, mentally urging Tara Lipinski or Michelle Kwan through triple Salchows and Hamill Camels.

"Oh God," he would say. "You should have seen this sixteen-year-old French girl. She was skating just incredibly, looked like she might even make the medals – which would've been a major upset – then she took a big fall on her final triple-toe. Oh, it was awful! I felt so bad."

His musical tastes were more predictable. He was a metalhead from way back, and I'd often arrive home to the pounding of Ratt, Poison or Bon Jovi on the stereo. Even here, though, he took a scholarly approach, spending hours searching the web for information on the groundbreaking band The New York Dolls, and their leader, Johnny Thunders. When you considered my own growing obsession with opera, I suppose we were confusing the hell out of our neighbors, *Tosca* one minute, Metallica the next. But we did have our meeting-ground – in grunge-era pioneers like Nirvana, Soundgarden and Pearl Jam (he loaned me a Courtney Love CD that I played obsessively).

The only sign of dissonance – besides the exiled shoes – was the contrast of our lifestyles. As a first-time entrepreneur, Tommy was the Puritan work ethic incarnate, waking at sunrise, working past nightfall, logging long hours at the computer without a break. My own habits were much more casual, and focused entirely around the writing of novels. This meant day jobs like housepainting and freelance journalism – but only enough to pay the bills. This meant Rollerblading to a café to compose over lattes, then blading home to watch late-night TV and play solitaire on my computer until the creative buzz wore off and I could sleep. And then, waking up whenever I felt like it.

It was an exciting time for me. I had gotten my hooks into a novel that contained my complete heart, plus all the grief I felt for my mother's death. It took place in a small opera company, and in doing the research I had arranged to cover the San Francisco Opera for a small South Bay newspaper. During the fall season, I spent two nights a week in The City, eating up the delights of big-time opera like a puppy chewing furniture. I even taught myself an aria – "Voi che sapete," from Mozart's *Marriage of Figaro* and sang it as I bladed home from the café.

It also didn't hurt that all of my good-looking female friends just adored dressing up for the opera. Alas, none of them were girlfriends, but I sure enjoyed showing up at the opera house with one babe after another on my arm.

Queen of them all was Robin, the finest-looking woman I've ever known – and charmingly oblivious of the fact. (To this day, her mechanic and I sit around letting out profound sighs, lamenting her escape to Milan with the new Italian husband.) Robin picked me up at my place, wearing a knit top that embraced her fashion-model torso like a coat of fuzzy paint. When I introduced her to Tommy, I thought he was going to blow a gasket.

I imagined that these occasional visits would bring a few rays of female sunshine into Tommy's self-inflicted prison. It probably just fed the fire. Here he was, weighed down with a mortgage, a new business, a crippled heart and a life-long struggle with substances. And here was Honus, who woke up at noon, worked a couple hours, then went to a café to produce beautiful, effortless works of art. To top it off, despite having no money for an Internet provider or health insurance, he goes to the opera with a different Miss California each week. It just isn't fair.

Like any miserable person, Tommy took to giving advice. My typical reply: "Okay, I'll think about it." But like most advice – givers, Tommy didn't like it when his advice was ignored.

EIGHTEEN

Dear Abby

Tommy's initial suggestions were not all bad, especially because he backed them up with gifts. The first two were a laser printer and an answering machine, exiled from Tommy's office for minor defects. The printer etched a faint gray line at the right of each page. The answering machine kept playing back a five-year-old message on the second line, even though the second line was no longer in use. I taped over it with Kiri Te Kanawa singing Mozart, so at least the nightly repetition would be pleasant.

This kind of reclamation was nothing new. I was the dog at the Silicon Valley table, waiting for high-tech crumbs. I had gone through several computers and never purchased one – the latest a hand-me-down from my sister's job at Hewlett-Packard.

Problem was, Tommy wanted me to soar along with him, Icarus-like, into the Internet heavens: a server, a browser, email, a scanner – my own web site! But all of these things involved cash layouts and monthly charges – and were, for me, completely unnecessary. Tommy spent the next two days pouting at my turndown, in a manly, brooding sort of way.

The all-encompassing, liver-picking poverty of the artistic life was entirely my choice – but I still needed to bitch about it. To me, the appropriate response to my complaints would have been an understanding nod and a sagacious commiseration like, "Wow, dude – that sucks!"

Tommy's mental process was more like, *Hmm, Honus has a problem – I will fix it for him!* "Have you thought about tech writing, Honus? What about temp work? There's lots of work in the malls around Christmas. Have you thought about getting a loan and going back for a master's?"

And then I would turn down his advice, and Tommy would spend the next two days pouting, in a manly, brooding sort of way. (*Why does Honus bring his problems to me if he's never going to take my advice?*) I was beginning to understand why he had so many problems with women.

The next stage was a long period of inscrutable household tension. I suspected a fatherly disappointment in my ne'er-do-well ways, but I could never be sure, because Tommy's self-driven anxieties and superhuman work schedule followed him around the house like a dark cloud.

Any artist will tell you, once you begin the mental construction of defenses for the things you do, you've already lost the battle. In the real world, there are no practical justifications for the creation of 500-page novels and surreal poems (nor should there be). The only workable strategy is to realize that some people will never get it, and go your merry way.

I began a campaign to avoid my own house, slipping out on morning paint jobs while Tommy sat chained to his computer, and not returning till late at night. I retrieved my old television from Anne's apartment and set it up in the den, with the result that Tommy and I would spend our midnight wind-downs in separate rooms, perhaps twenty feet from each other, often watching the same channel. The secession was complete.

No distance, however, could keep me from Tommy's re-entry into the world of substances. I awoke to his smoker's hack, which sounded like an old, beat-up engine starting up on a cold morning. After that it was coffee and cigarettes all morning, followed by a six-pack of light beer in the late afternoon and evening, and then a pre-sleep joint in front of the tube as he watched Jay Leno.

Returning from an evening of novelizing – what should have been the most satisfying hour of my day – I would sit on the porch to take off my blades and prepare for the gauntlet. Inside I would find either Drunk Tommy, bouncing from one intense, unfocused mood to another; or Deadhead Tommy, letting out terrier yelps at Jay's nightly monologue. I think I preferred Deadhead Tommy, but I longed for a housemate who would just stay the same person for a while.

The growing distance turned our occasional conversations into major events. This generally occurred about once every other week, when Tommy would call out as I passed in the hallway.

"Hey, Honus. Do you have a minute to talk? Here, have a seat." Then he would get that professorly look, like he did before pre-game pep talks, and announce, "I really need your help, Honus. The kitchen has become a real pig sty, and it needs a thorough going-over. What I need you to do is scrub down the counters, then the sink, then give the floor a good mopping with that Clean-All stuff under the sink. Does that sound okay?"

I developed a fantasy version of these little conferences, a teleplay that goes something like this:

TOMMY

(Reaching into fridge for carton of eggs.)
Hey, Honus. Could you clean the kitchen this weekend?

HONUS

(Reading sports section.)
Sure, no prob. Hey, how 'bout those Giants, huh?

Fade to black.

Fat chance. Tommy was too fond of the rhetoric of administration, and talked exactly like the asshole managers of my short-lived office career. (Never an actual yes-or-no question, always "I need you to…" as if the big prick's mental health depended on your cooperation.)

The other irritation was Tommy's Felix Unger complex. Believe me, I've seen the depths of bachelor housekeeping, and ours was nowhere close. In addition, none of the few coffee stains and counter-crumbs were left by yours truly, because yours truly was so paranoid about his housemate's judgments that he cleaned up his messes two seconds after making them, and couldn't have left a dirty dish in the sink if you held a gun to his head.

So what did I do? I cleaned the kitchen.

But even with the high tides of tension, Tommy and I found our meeting places. We were both unabashed liberals, and spent the news hours cussing out the Republican dickweeds, who would kick out an elected President over a couple of blowjobs.

We also had Stevie Becker's sports mementos. Stevie and Tammy were ensconced in an apartment, waiting out escrow on their new house, and had left Stevie's miniature Cooperstown in our guest room. I'd hear Tommy on the phone, talking to Stevie about our recent activities. "Yeah, me and Honus went down to the ballfield for some batting practice. I'll tell ya, that Willie Mays bat has one helluva sweet spot."

"Yeah," I'd shout. "Bummer about that inside pitch."

"Don't worry," said Tommy. "Little bit of caulking and it'll be good as new. And the crack is nowhere near the autograph. I did tell Honus, though, that we shouldn't a been hitting rocks with it."

Our best, most evil prank went sadly untried. The idea was to buy a basketball, identical to Stevie's Michael Jordan-autographed model, then forge the signature and show up at Stevie's place, casually bouncing it on the porch.

"Hey Stevie! Wanna go shoot some hoops?"

The only complete relief arrived in the spring, when Tommy and I returned to the softball field. We joined a "just for fun" coed league, and the presence of the both of us on a diamond had a remarkable healing effect.

Perhaps the best testament to our mutual dedication arrived during the league playoffs. I had a theater review that night, but, thinking I had plenty of time to spare, I got a ride to the game with Tommy. Naturally, the games took forever, and you'd have a tough time deciding who made the greater sacrifice: Tommy, who handed me the keys to his cherished two-year-old Camaro and hitched a ride home with a friend; or me, who arrived at the theater in full softball regalia.

My favorite image from that season, however, arrived a few weeks before, when we made a post-game trip to my poet friend Rob's house so I could pick up some mail. Rob walked me back to the street, where we found Tommy, dressed in his letter-perfect

Barons uniform, Detroit Tigers cap and reflector sunglasses, leaning on the hood of his double-parked Camaro and lighting a cigarette.

"Wow!" said Rob. "You look like the reason for the downfall of communism!"

NINETEEN

The Enunciator of Our Dreams

My poet friend Calder described an acquaintance as a "shadow artist." I asked her what that meant, and she explained it as a term she found in a book called *The Artist's Way* by Julia Cameron. It describes a person who has a strong creative instinct, perhaps even genuine talent, but who, for various reasons – lack of discipline, fear of rejection, social or financial pressures – fails to pursue it. They often try to fill the void by befriending real artists, but they are not to be trusted. Though they begin as wholehearted supporters of the artist's work, eventually the envy kicks in and they become closet saboteurs.

I soon stumbled on a way to test this hypothesis on Tommy. I had joined a blues band, and it became obvious that the lead guitarist was tired of hosting rehearsals in his crowded living room. I asked Tommy if we could use his garage, and he seemed downright excited by the idea. He paid us the ultimate compliment by leaving his hovel to peek in on our first rehearsal. A couple hours later, once the band had packed up and left, I went to Tommy's office for a review.

"Are you kidding me, man? You guys kicked ass! I was groovin' the whole time back here. That lead guitarist rocks, and you're great on drums, Honus. I mean, you know, you run into a lot of guys who 'play some drums,' but how many of them actually turn out to be good?"

That was the peak of our critical acclaim. Over the weeks, I could see the shadow working its way through his head like a cockroach – the vague irritation when I asked if I could back the Camaro out of the garage, muttered comments about the guitar amps stashed against the wall, and the empty beer bottle left on top of the dryer. *Great, here's my ne'er-do-well housemate doing yet another fun thing while I'm stuck back here all day working on this fucking sign – and strange people wandering through the house every Tuesday night.*

Our bassist, Jon, ever the detector of bad vibes, asked, "Hey, Honus, does your housemate not like having us here? He seems kinda… edgy."

He also never again came to watch us. I asked if we could move rehearsals to the lead singer's house.

Another bad omen arrived soon after. Tommy had mentioned "helping out around the house" as a term of my tenancy, and I had foolishly agreed without asking for specifics. Tommy began making reference to my "lack of initiative" without mentioning what exactly he wanted me to do. I finally got him to draw up a list. A few of them involved arrangements with outside entities – replacing the fixtures in the kitchen, for instance, or getting new glass for my bedroom window. This made me nervous, because there was no way I could afford to pay for these things.

We managed to duck out of this conflict in the usual weird, unspoken way. I did all the other chores, and Tommy eventually transferred the cash repairs to his own to-do list. And never did them.

I exited my bedroom one morning to find Tommy at the kitchen table, dressed in a sweater vest like a young Bing Crosby and looking remarkably chipper.

"Mornin'," I offered.

"Hi," he said. "Hey, how'd you like to play shortstop on my new softball team?"

"Company team?" I asked.

"The Barons."

"No shit!" I said.

"No shit. I've been running into the old players lately – Stevie Hammer, Gilly, Greg Macy, had breakfast with Stevie Becker just now. Every last one of them wants to get the team back together, but I'm not gonna do it without you. So, are you in?"

"Fuck yes I am! When do we play?"

"We're practicing this Saturday at Henry Schmidt, then we play the summer season at Double River, beginning in June."

What Vero Beach was to the Dodgers, what Scottsdale is to the Giants, that's what Henry Schmidt was to the Barons. It was an unassuming dirt diamond in Santa Clara with one of those elliptical chain-link backstops and a stand of trees in deep right that made long fly balls a lumberjacking experience. It wasn't much, but it was ours, the place where we resurfaced each spring to work the old dances back into our feet. It was also where Tommy put us through an infield boot camp of oddly spinning, vicious grounders, and where Greg Macy always sent two or three balls over the right-field grove into neighboring yards.

We had played in the winter league one year, and quickly realized we never would again. It wasn't even the rain-soaked games or the year-old injuries. We needed an opportunity to miss the game – and to rediscover it on that first sunny Saturday in March. Sometimes I think I enjoyed practicing the game more than playing it. When you added up the motions, you could squeeze more softball into two hours of practice than five regular games.

You can imagine the level of spring-training fever brought on by a year-long drought of Barons softball. Tommy and I were welcomed to the Henry Schmidt parking lot by all the familiar sounds and expressions: Stevie Becker's morning throat-clearings, Gilly's relaxed grin, Rico Carlo's droll commentary, brother-in-law Barry's silent, Secret Service entrance. And Tommy's keynote address.

"Gentlemen. What a pleasure to be back on the green green grass of Henry Schmidt with the bases full of... Barons! This is gonna be one helluva reunion tour. Now get out there and let's see if we remember how to play this game."

I stood at short fending off Tommy's squirrelly grounders, then looked around at a veritable Barons all-star roster. It may, in fact, have been a little too exciting. Toward the end of infield I made a sudden move and kicked off my cardiac arrhythmia – a locked-in overdrive of 140 beats per minute. I went to lie on a bench until it harrumphed back down.

I snuck into left field to shag some flies for batting practice (the best aerobic workout in softball). Then Tommy called me in and tossed balls over the outside corner so I could whack them into right field. After that, I asked him to get a little wild so I could practice my two-strike swing, then to groove some over the middle for my power stroke.

The way the balls were pouncing from the bat reaffirmed a goal I had already set for myself: after a four-year drought, it was time for the old veteran to go for another MVP award. That achievement generally came with two statistics – batting average and RBI – and I knew that Greg Macy would offer some stiff competition.

Despite all the time off, we had all been playing elsewhere, and handled our first game with all pistons firing. Being back between Gilly at third and Johnny Silva at second was like coming home, and my offensive routine was amazingly unchanged: single to right, dodge Stevie Becker's left-field bullets, then score on the Greg Macy homer or single-up-the-middle.

The only big change was Mitch Kashahara, my coed league shortstop, whose height and lack of seniority had relegated him to first (I had actually offered to play outfield, but Tommy's sense of tradition wouldn't allow it). Mitch batted leadoff, a perfect match for his speed and up-the-middle prowess. We asked Stevie Becker to take his hardball-battered body to right-center, and shifted Barry (years older, but not half so battered) to right.

We spent that first game smacking around a team that carried all the markings of Double River debutantes: too many pull hitters, uniforms a little too neat, and batters who took a little too much time taking breaths between pitches. We celebrated at a Tex-Mex place in Sunnyvale, where we spent most of our time discussing Gilly, Greg and the two Stevies' favorite sport: golf.

"Oh, I'll give you two strokes on Santa Theresa. Those long, hilly par-fives – I will nail you on those!"

"Dude! No shit, I shot a seventy-nine there just last week. Are you gonna beat that? Besides, I've watched you on the greens, Gilly. I've seen better strokes in a preschool swim class."

"At least I get to the greens, Stevie…"

"Oh!"

Tommy and I shared a secret smile, recalling our disastrous attempt at a nine-holer the summer before. As for the girls – April, who had recently become Mrs. Macy, and Shauna, who was back with Gilly, still waiting – they looked fabulously bored, finding it hard to believe that they had now become widows to two sports at once.

Tommy and I developed a pleasant Friday evening routine. We would drive a mile north to Stevie Becker's house, where we would find him dashing from room to room, looking for some missing piece of his uniform. Minutes later, we would be cruising 101 with both windows down (Tommy's preference) and Stevie would shout questions through the rush of air.

"So what do you think of the Giants this year, Honus?! Think we got a chance?"

"Yeah, sure!" I said. "Gotta get those young pitchers goin', though, and we definitely need to keep Barry off the disabled list!"

"Yeah, I think that's the thing! How's the business goin', Tommy!?"

"Pretty good! Doin' a huge sign for the NorCom building in Milpitas! Lots of nasty little specs, but major checks on the way!"

"I'll tell you what!" said Stevie. "Ol' Honus is gonna win a Pulitzer, have his name on some big-ass marquee designed by

Tommy, and then I'm gonna be his agent and get fifteen percent of everything! We're gonna be BIG, gentlemen!"

Stevie was full of shit, but he was also the enunciator of our dreams. It was hard to maintain your pessimism with Stevie shouting sunny visions from the back seat – even for Tommy, who had turned pessimism into a lifestyle. It also lowered the friction in our household. We couldn't always agree with each other, but we could always agree with Stevie.

We had a good season. There were two good young Latino teams – one of the trash-talking variety, one not. We had the pleasure of beating the jerks in the semis before losing to the good guys in the finals. Our conquerors were a scrappy bunch, the kind of team that plays smart, tough defense, drills pesky singles through the infield, and takes extra bases with well-executed slides. One of those slides upended me on a double-play turn. I clambered to my feet and told the runner, "Good slide." He gave me a pat on the shoulder on his way to the dugout. There are times when softball can be downright civilized.

But that wasn't enough for me. When I saw several of them outside the clubhouse, trying out their championship T-shirts, I stopped to offer my appreciation.

"You know, there's a lot of teams out here that win championships, but not many that play the game right. You guys play the game right. So, congratulations."

I shook hands all around, but couldn't help noticing their puzzled looks. Such displays of sportsmanship – especially from a white guy to a Latino team – were not exactly common at Double River. All the more reason to make the effort, I thought.

I had exactly the kind of season I'd hoped for, hitting the .700 mark and nudging out Greg Macy on most of the stats (largely because Greg missed four games). A couple weeks into the fall season, Tommy conducted one of his post-game gatherings and handed me the MVP award, a custom-made plaque with a red Barons logo against a black background. It will, most assuredly, never end up in a landfill. It also signaled, in an unexpected way, the end of the household frictions between myself and Tommy Folgett.

TWENTY

Round One

It was a sunny Saturday morning in October. I had showered and was sitting around in my layabout clothes, gazing out the big front window. I wondered when our liquidambar would begin its turn to russet reds and tangerines. I also wondered when it would stop dropping those spiky pods we called "dingleberries," the raking of which constituted my principal household chore. I didn't even notice that Tommy had escaped his lair and was standing at the entrance to the living room. He got my attention by clearing his throat. I hit the pause button on the CD player.

"Hey," he said. "How's it goin'?"

"Pretty good," I half-yawned. "Just getting in my morning grunge. Pearl Jam, man, they are the best."

"Yeah. Much as I enjoy that new band – Creed? – it's a little spooky how much their lead singer sounds like Eddie Vedder. Um… " Tommy ran a hand through his unwashed hair. "You got a few minutes to talk?"

Oh boy – here we go.

"Yeah, sure."

Tommy settled on an armchair across the room, fifteen feet away. He leaned forward and rested his arms on his knees.

"Well, here's the news report, Honus. I'm giving up on my business. The cash flow has finally caught up with me, so I got a job with a sign company. I'll be working eight to five – but I'll still work evenings on my business, mostly developing my website. This presents a bit of a predicament, because there'll be even more of a premium on my time. I'm gonna need some help from you, specifically in putting a little more initiative into maintaining things around the house..."

Blame it on the MVP award, blame it on Tommy's predilection for talking about his business as if it were some kind of charity, toward which we should all be contributing, but I felt the sudden need to be contrary.

"Well, you see, this is the same problem we had before, Tommy. I'd like to show initiative, but it's hard for me to know exactly what needs to be done, because I'm not the owner of the house. Can you give me some examples?"

Tommy looked confused. For nine years, we had cultivated a rather military relationship. He was the manager, I was the shortstop, and I pretty much did what I was told (eerily similar to my drummer-singer relationship with Melody Marshall). I had allowed this hierarchy to carry over to the household, where I invariably assented to Tommy's requests rather than deal with the hassle of an argument. Now, all of a sudden, his shortstop had refused to cover second on a double play, and Tommy didn't know where to throw the ball.

"Um, well…" he said. "I suppose I could think of a few. The fixtures in the kitchen still need replacing. Then there's the cracked window in your room, especially with the rainy season coming on – and I'd sure like to get that den painted someday, it looks pretty awful."

"Well," I said. "Perhaps I wasn't very clear on this before, but I assumed we had agreed that the fixtures and the window required outside services, and would best be handled by the owner of the house. And certainly, I shouldn't be expected to lay out cash for such things, because they do constitute improvements to the property. As for the painting, you've got me in a tough spot, because that is, after all, what I do for a living. I'm sure you'd feel the same about graphic design. We could exchange for rent, if you like."

I could see the blood rising in Tommy's face, his gestures becoming agitated. I hadn't seen him like this since Craig Scarlet literally fell asleep in left field, as a line drive zipped past his head.

"I thought we had an understanding when you moved in, Honus, that four hundred dollars is a pretty goddamn good rent, so I thought we'd agreed that you would help keep the place up. The most irritating thing for me is having to point out whenever the kitchen is a mess when it should be pretty fuckin' obvious to anyone, when you should just clean it without me havin' to say a goddamn thing!"

This is where my MVP demeanor came in. As Tommy's voice grew louder, as he began to throw in expletives, I could feel the adrenaline building in my limbs – but inside, I was calm. I held the bat loosely in my hands, bounced on the pads of my feet, and waited for that pitch on the outside corner. Besides, I had a trump card in my back pocket.

"That's the other problem," I said. "Whenever I use the kitchen, I take great pains to clean up every little mess immediately after I make it. Every dish goes directly into the dishwasher. I do that for a reason. I've had lots of housemates before, and believe me, it's the only way you can stay clear of conflict. And then I come out here some Sunday morning and look at this bright, shiny kitchen – the cleanest-looking kitchen I have ever lived around – and you tell me it's a pig sty. All I can figure is you must be hallucinating."

Oh, that pressed a button. I was actually referring to his Felix Unger fussiness, but Tommy thought I was talking about substances. He shot out of his chair and let loose with a full volley.

"Now you're getting personal, you ungrateful son-of-a-bitch! I take you in, give you this great fucking rent – and you throw shit on me, you throw a great big pile of shit on me! Well fuck you very much! I'm under a lot of goddamn pressure, and I don't need some so-called fucking friend dumping on my ass! All I ask is a little help around the house and this is what I get? Well fuck you!"

That seemed to be the end of the rant. I sat there on the sofa, trying to quell my anger. I pulled my trump card from my pocket, held it there in my fingers – but it wouldn't work unless I delivered it in a calm tone of voice.

"I'm giving my thirty-day notice. I'll be moving out by November 7."

That button was even hotter than the first. Tommy exploded all over again, and this time I felt free to join in, the two of us standing at opposite ends of the room and tossing every f-word, s-word, p-, a- and c-word we could think of. When we finally ran out, we both stomped out of the room at once, Tommy down the hallway, me to the front porch with a mighty door-slam.

Once I ceased muttering obscenities, I realized I was in a touchy situation. I was stuck outside in my bare feet, without my car keys. I thought of sneaking into the garage for my cleats, but instead I just sat there, gazing into the harsh light, anger oscillating my limbs. It was nice, though, that Tommy had decided not to come out and heap further abuse on me, and that the front lawn contained not one dingleberry. I felt strangely powerful.

All the next week, Tommy and I crept around each other like we were human land mines. I had my movements carefully mapped out: a three-foot crossing to the bathroom and back, a twenty-foot dash to the front door. I spent my evenings at a late-closing Starbucks in Willow Glen, writing at the outdoor tables until they came to take them away. Anything so I could avoid that godawful house. I didn't know where I was going to move yet, but it would have been preferable to live in a cardboard box atop the Himalayas.

I had a Saturday-morning date with a friend, so I couldn't avoid passing through the kitchen where Tommy was eating breakfast. I tried to drop a quick "Good morning" and leave, but Tommy stopped me. He looked so feeble I thought he was sick.

"Hey, Honus. Can I ask you something?"

"Uh... sure," I said.

Tommy stood and put a hand on my shoulder. His eyes were bloodshot; his voice trembled.

"Look, Honus, I... understand why you want to leave, and I'm really sorry about all those things we said last Saturday. But... I can't do this without you, Honus. Would you consider stickin' around a while longer? I really need you to stay."

The word 'need' was no longer rhetorical. My hard-ass manager, tormentor of enemy batters, the reason for the downfall of communism, was fighting back tears. What could I say? I said yes.

TWENTY-ONE

Balance of Power

Tommy's plea created a palpable shift in the household. I no longer had to operate under the assumption that my tenancy was a nuisance – because Tommy had revealed it as a necessity. In fact, it was now he who tiptoed around, trying his best not to ruffle his housemate's feathers.

I took immediate steps toward positive reinforcement. Even though Tommy had withdrawn his complaints about the kitchen, I scrubbed that sucker down, and then I cleaned the bathroom. Plus, after I vacuumed my room, I continued on to wherever its cord would take me: the living room, the hallway, Tommy's office.

While working out on Tommy's neglected weight machine, I noticed the scars and smudges along the den walls. I found a gallon of leftover paint in the garage and gave the room a new coat, exulting in Tommy's look of surprise when he returned home.

Tommy had mentioned an overgrown lemon tree in the side yard, so I borrowed my dad's pruning saw and had at it – and then at the sprawling oak that was threatening to take over the back yard. I dragged the limbs out to curbside, filling up two parking

THE LEGENDARY BARONS · Michael J. Vaughn

spaces. The following day was Halloween, so I stuffed an old ski suit with leaves, tied shoes to the legs and left it protruding from the pile like a corpse. I added an old softball bat, lathered up with ketchup.

Soon after Thanksgiving, I rescued a painted wooden snowman from Tommy's scrap heap, placed it on the porch and strung up some Christmas lights. It wasn't much, compared to our neighbors, but it was nice to return from my writing sessions to the Vegas-style lights flashing around our cypress bush.

This streak of volunteerism was accompanied by yet another creative renaissance. I had grown fond of taking walks along the beach near my dad's house in Aptos, where the El Niño storms had kicked up all kinds of debris – including frosted glass. I sometimes found a hundred pieces on a single trip, and I began to envision a character who was obsessed with the stuff. To write the character, I had to become obsessed with the stuff myself, so I went to the beach three or four times a week. I took great pleasure in telling my dad – a no-nonsense Midwest type – that I was doing research; that technically, this was my job. I found my setting during a trip to the Oregon Coast, and gave myself three whole days off after finishing my opera novel before starting *Frosted Glass*.

My other pursuits were tooling along, as well. I was actually being paid to be the fiction editor of a new literary journal, and the blues band began playing gigs at a coffeehouse. Even my house painting was artistic; I was doing a Victorian interior in San Francisco, complete with ornate moldings and a sky-blue oval ceiling.

I had a good fall season with the Barons – no MVP season, but no one else had one, either. We finished at .500 and failed to make the playoffs, a rare occurrence. But I was so happy with my artistic and domestic bliss that I really didn't care. I still had an occasional notion to look for another place, but these were tempered by thoughts of my cheap rent and Tommy's heartfelt request.

In late February, as the weather began to pull out of its deep, wet winter, our thoughts turned back to softball. A week before our first practice, Tommy pulled me aside for our first household discussion since the Missiles of October.

"Honus, things at the job have been going really well, and I'm starting to look into expanding my home office. There's no rush, but do you think you could start looking for another place to live?"

TWENTY-TWO

The Legendary Duke

In essence, Tommy was asking me to leave on his terms when he had denied me the chance to leave on mine. But it worked out well – a little too well, if you asked Tommy. A week later, when I told him I had found a place and would be moving at the end of March, he seemed disturbed. Here was Honus, continuing to sail through life, while he had to constantly struggle.

Calder and Al, the publishers of the literary journal, were moving to Chicago, and needed a live-in cat-sitter while they went off house-hunting in Illinois. Before they left, I helped them fill a large rental dumpster with the non-essentials of their 25-year residency. The comedy came from their differing definitions of "non-essential." Al would sit on a crate in the storage shed, sorting through boxes until he filled up a trash barrel, then I would lug the barrel to the dumpster and empty it out. Calder would arrive soon after to pick through the pile like a homeless person, salvaging any photo, poem or knick-knack that might someday land a spot in the Smithsonian.

I would eventually string this and a handful of other house-sitting gigs into three months of rent-free existence, during which I saved up cash for my next long-term residence. Meanwhile, taking hacks at a rained-on practice at Henry Schmidt, I came to an interesting conclusion – an inkling so strong I had to verbalize it to Johnny Silva, who waited on deck.

"Johnny, I've used up all my breaks for a while. This season, I'm going to have to scratch and scrape for every base hit."

Call it self-fulfilling prophecy, but the karmic cycles of softball are real, and you had best pay attention when they send you messages. The trick is to hang in there, and keep the lows from getting too deep.

I also had some off-field distractions – good ones. Over Christmas, my opera novel won a $3,000 award from the local arts council. Two days later, my car blew a valve, and I bought a car from a friend – for $3,000.

What I never noticed about my friend's car was how sexy it was – a burgundy '88 Nissan 300ZX with a T-top. The day after I got my insurance, I drove to Half Moon Bay, took off the T-panels, lit a cigar and drove to Santa Cruz with *Madama Butterfly* blasting from the speakers. I had found a new hobby.

A month later, I met a tall, lovely actress named Debi and enjoyed a courtship of small, poetic gestures. Whenever I saw her, I gave her a piece of frosted glass. She used florist wire to dangle the pieces from the edge of her lampshade. As the weeks went by, our creation began to resemble a solar system of tiny, translucent planets.

Debi had a beautiful body, and I spent my nights checking various tall-girl fantasies off my mental list. She told me that I had "opened her up" in ways she had never experienced before. That comment, along with a menagerie of two dogs and two cats in a two-bedroom flat, should have sent me screaming from the room. I chose to ignore the warning signs, but I did predict to a friend that it would be over in three months. I was right on the money. She worshipped me for two months, nit-picked me for a third, then ended it with an email signed "The Once-Again Single Psycho Bitch From Hell."

Regardless, I will always owe Debi a debt of gratitude, because it was she who won me an audience with Duke Snider.

Mitch and Dawna held the world's most perfect wedding at Crocker Mansion in Hillsborough. I can still picture the Duke of Flatbush, head of white hair, spectacles, bad knees and all, escorting his beautiful golden-haired daughter down a winding stone staircase that looked like it had been shipped in by Disney.

Debi was late, victim of a play opening and my bad directions, but when she arrived she was a vision, draped in a long dress of purple velvet. When we hit the ballroom for our first-ever dance as a couple, it seemed like we had been doing it for years. (She had, in fact, been pursuing dance professionally, until she, like the Duke, lost out to knee troubles.)

The groom, who should have been overwhelmed with other issues, made a particular point of introducing me to his new father-in-law, but I found myself in an awkward position. I was dying to talk baseball with him, but it seemed like the least appropriate subject for the occasion. Thus, after a handshake and the usual pleasantries, the conversation ground quickly to a halt. Duke turned his eyes to the dance floor, where a squad of youngsters was assembling a bunny-hop.

Debi jumped in. "Are those your grandchildren?"

In one easy stroke, she had landed on Duke's favorite subject. For the next ten minutes, he ran down the list – this one playing soccer, that one just starting kindergarten – eyes filling with affection. It was a genuine audience with one of the greats, and I owe that one to Debi for life.

Afterward, we drifted outside and discovered the genetic forces behind Mitch's shortstopping prowess. Several of Mitch's relatives, from a four-year-old nephew to a 50-year-old aunt, had found a soft "safety" baseball and were winging it around the courtyard like some Japanese coed version of the '55 Brooklyn Dodgers.

(This was hardly Duke's introduction to Japanese culture. The Dodgers toured Japan in the early '60s, and after the final out he endeared himself to the entire country by taking off most of his

THE LEGENDARY BARONS · Michael J. Vaughn

uniform and leaving it in center field for the fans to take home as souvenirs.)

Our final vision came at the front of the mansion, where a hundred guests had gathered with small champagne-bottle containers of bubble-blowing liquid. When the happy couple made their exit, they were greeted with a veritable Lawrence Welk whirlwind.

Mitch's entrance into baseball royalty was, in short, a Hall-of-Fame occasion, certain to turn the head of a fellow shortstop who was already showing signs of straying from the flock.

TWENTY-THREE

Batter Blues

Before our first game, Tommy gathered us around and delivered a stunner: Shauna and Gilly were getting married. The Baroness finally had her wish.

I suppose that bit of news was still skulking around in my head during my first at-bat, but it really shouldn't have mattered. Getting a look at my size, the pitcher tried to slip one by on the outside corner, and I drilled it – right to the second baseman. My second at-bat, same thing. My third time up, I got impatient, trying to take a pitch on the inside half and push it the other way. I got exactly what I deserved, a weak-ass chopper to the pitcher.

Everybody goes oh-fer once in a while, but come week two, the pattern continued. My first time up, I hit one a couple feet foul down the right field line, then followed with a strong grounder to the first baseman. My second at-bat, I hit a soft liner over the second baseman's head, only to see the right fielder pull a nifty head-long dive and snip it away, inches above the grass. My third at-bat, I pushed another inside pitch and grounded weakly to second.

It appeared that my inklings about a tough season were bearing fruit. But then the gods of softball got downright cruel. When I came up for my fourth at-bat, I had speedy Gilly on third with one out and a slim two-run lead. *Fine*, I thought. *Since I'm so goddamned good at grounding out to second, I'll do just that and at least get the run in.* The pitcher gave me my pitch, I slapped it to second, then ran down the line, clapping my hands at my small victory. Problem being, Gilly was still at third! What's worse, he wandered too far from the bag and got picked off by a throw from the first baseman.

I couldn't remember the last time Gilly had made a baserunning error, much less two in five seconds. When I asked him, he said he thought there were two outs – which made no damn sense, since with two outs he would have been going as soon as I made contact. I walked out to short thinking, *That's what getting engaged does for your brain cells.*

I resolved to keep an even keel. As long as I hit the ball low, hard, and to the right, good things would happen. Then I showed up for game number three and found myself batting seventh.

A good manager knows that hitters will have their streaks and slumps. A hitter with a proven record will eventually come back around; an unproven player hitting unusually well is best left where he is, because that's where he's comfortable. I recall the rookie year of A's shortstop Mike Bordick, who began the year hitting better than he had in his entire minor-league career. But his manager, Tony LaRussa, refused to move him from the ninth spot, and he finished the season with a .300 average.

Tommy had always followed the same theory, waiting seven, eight games – often an entire season – before demoting a scuffling veteran. In my case, there were additional factors: I was not hitting the ball badly, just in the wrong spots; I had been our number-two hitter for most of a decade; and I was twelve games removed from an MVP season. Having just been dropped five spots after two games, I came to an obvious conclusion: Tommy was fucking with me, and looking to get back the authority he had lost in October.

So what did I do? I did my job. And though the third game brought more ground-outs, I started a late-inning rally with a single up the middle. And I didn't take my slump into the field. In fact, although the years had taken a step from me, they gave me a store of knowledge that more than made up for it. I knew when to "eat" the ball, how to call off an outfielder when two of them converged on a fly ball, when to get the force at second and forget the double play, how to read Tommy's patterns and get a break on an inside or outside pitch.

And I also had company. Johnny Silva, finally recovered from an arm injury, was nailing line drive after line drive, directly into our opponents' gloves. He was often called out before he could get out of the batter's box.

Johnny worked for Nike, and his employer's rah-rah slogans sometimes crept into his on-field declarations. I had to at least provide a little ribbing. One night, after a bad call from an umpire, Johnny shouted, "It doesn't matter! We gotta suck it up, man! The team that's right is the one with the most runs at the end of the game!"

"Jesus, Johnny," I said. "Sometimes you sound like a commercial for *Sports Illustrated.*"

Johnny pretty much ignored this, but not Tommy. On the ride home, we were discussing the overall flatness of the team.

"Well, it would help," said Tommy, "if you supported your teammates when they're firing up the team, instead of making fucking jokes about *Sports Illustrated.*"

I was in no mood to agree. "What am I supposed to do, leave my brain at home?"

"Yeah," said Tommy. "That would be a start."

A week before my move, I arrived home to find Tommy eating his favorite meal: beef stroganoff and steamed broccoli.

"You know, Honus, I don't think you should hit to the right so much. You've got a great natural swing, and I know you've got power. I think you'd be better off going for the center of the field and just letting loose."

Nothing like hitting advice from the weakest hitter in Barons history. And you know? I took it. Perhaps it was the unappealing prospect of absorbing one more week of silent scorn if I said no. Perhaps it was the desire to leave the house on a positive note. But here's what it really was: if I took his advice, I was officially off the hook. I was just following orders, and whatever ensued was Tommy Folgett's own damn fault.

Over the next few weeks, I hit for more power, I hit to the center, and succeeded in bringing my average up to the level of a mediocre player. Tommy rewarded me by dropping me to the ninth spot in the lineup. The only hitter behind me was Tommy Folgett.

TWENTY-FOUR

Stealing Home

After my final flare-up with Debi, and after my friends Al and Calder moved to Chicago, I began a long and perilous search for shelter.

I asked a friend if I could rent out her guest room, just while I looked for a new place. She made certain to ask for her neighborhood's lofty market rate, then spent my entire stay making it clear how much she was looking forward to my departure. I learned, in short, that ours was a limited friendship.

After a month, I moved into a two-bedroom apartment with an amiable divorced man, his weekends-only three-year-old son, and his parrot. Three weeks later, the landlord discovered the bad debts on my credit record and demanded a massive additional deposit.

What he didn't know was, I had been reading a history of the Donner Party. Compared to that level of suffering, what was one crusty old landlord? I paid an apologetic farewell to my roommate, picked up a spare tent at my little sister's house, and vowed to make the circuit of state and regional parks until the

Silicon Valley real estate market let drop one moderately priced situation.

On my first night, I tried three state parks on the coast and found them full-up. I showed up at my father's house in Aptos and asked if I could use the guest room for the night. He rubbed the back of his neck as he considered the question, as if after 37 years he was still not sure if he had taught me the value of self-reliance. I stood on the welcome mat, shrinking by the second, until he relented.

The next morning, I drove along Monterey Bay until I found a campsite at Sunset Beach, near Watsonville. I stayed there four days, grateful for coin-operated showers and miles-long walks on the beach. My freelance work and continuing room-search meant an hour-and-a-half drive to my cybercafe in the Valley, but I didn't mind. My plan, for the while, was working.

The weekend brought more full campsites, but I discovered a passable alternative. My little sister offered me her small camper, which sat on blocks in the driveway. Not wanting to disturb my sister's family when I arrived late at night, I would order a salad at a nearby Denny's, then adjourn to the restroom for my pre-slumber pee and toothbrushing.

Softball became, simultaneously, more and less important. More, because it was the only place I felt at home. Less, because, in the face of such an arduous daily existence, how could I care about winning or losing a silly game?

The Barons and I continued our mediocrity. We failed to make the spring playoffs, and seemed entirely uninspired heading into the summer. I continued to follow Tommy's advice, continued to hit a mundane .500, and continued to resent Double River's toxic combination of weak umpires and petty, intense, lazy softball players.

The only oasis was my Sunnyvale team, where I continued hitting .700, chasing fly balls and enjoying myself. There was also an unexpected bonus: Robin and Shane, a brother-brother umpire combo who were friends from high school.

At the end of August, I checked into Henry Cowell Redwoods, a state park in the Santa Cruz Mountains, and spent a week in a forest of tan oak and madrone. The guys at the neighboring campsite conducted all-night belching contests, but the park had hot showers, the previous residents left me a jam-jar filled with roses, and I spent my evenings in nearby Felton, where I had spent a summer ten years before. I was hanging around the old pizza parlor, checking in with my dad on a pay phone, when I spotted a flyer for a room in Boulder Creek, ten miles down the road.

It was my long-awaited jackpot.

I met the two tenants – a costume designer and an architect of stunt-bike parks – and was shown the room, a little old and musty, but overlooking a creek and a grove of redwoods. They called back a week later and asked if they could take a fourth roommate as well, which would drop my rent to an astonishing $250.

I said yes. The next day, I drove by to sign my agreement, pay my deposit, and meet roommate number four, a bubbly coed from UC Santa Cruz. I tooled into town and found a funky cafe, where I could spend all those writing hours freed up by my new, barely visible cost of living. As a final test, I took my future commute down the sweeping redwood curves of Highway 9, and found it perfectly suited to my sexy old sportscar. I ended the day at my sister's camper, where I enjoyed the finest sleep of an unsettled year.

TWENTY-FIVE

Hell Week

The league's most-hated team was Los Tigres, a band of trash-talking punks who had been tormenting us for a couple years now. They made me long for the Shnakes, a team whose players were nicknamed "Diamondback" and "Anaconda," who wrapped a rubber boa around the dugout fence – a team we hated with a vengeance. But compared to what we felt for Los Tigres, that seemed good-natured, civilized.

Los Tigres were not only premium assholes, they seemed to have a hex on us. A month before, they came into their last at-bat seven runs behind and methodically pecked away at us with line drives until their hits and our errors gave them the ballgame.

Their relentless pushing of our buttons played a part, too. But this time, I had a strategy. In the third inning, their chubby shortstop refused to leave second base, because he disagreed with the umpire's call. I spoke to him like a scolding father.

"The umpire called you out. Your job now is to go sit with your teammates."

This naturally inspired all kinds of invective from El Gordo. I responded by laughing and returning to my position. The next batter, a shorter, athletic-looking kid, hustled out a double and finished with a well-done hook-slide. I immediately classified him as one of the good guys, and stayed at the bag to chat.

"Hey, nice huss, man."

"Thanks."

"Boy, that shortstop of yours is testy, ain't he?"

"Yeah," he smiled. "He's kind of a hothead."

"'Salright. My pitcher acts the same way."

That small conversation helped me to chip away at the angry team-wide facade of Los Tigres. It also made me feel more human, less stressed out about the game.

The rest of the Barons, however, were not doing too well, especially when Los Tigres, down by that same seven runs, began their last at-bat with five straight singles. Then we generously contributed a couple of errors, one of them mine, an earth-hugging grounder that looked for sure like it was going to pop up on a rock and hit me in the face. Instead, it stuck to the ground like a bullet train and choo-chooed right under my glove.

Several batters later, we were in deep shit: two outs, tying run at the plate – sphincters tightening all across the field. But not mine. When the next batter hit a grounder to my right, I was on it like Patrick Roy on a loose puck, pinning it to the ground, fighting for a grip and flinging it to first from my knees. I got him by a step and the Barons let out a righteous roar.

We hung out in the parking lot for a half-hour, watching tiny burrowing owls skitter around under a full moon. Stevie Becker rested on the hood of Tommy's Camaro, relishing our narrow escape.

"Them Latino boys came that close to kicking us in the balls again. But they didn't!"

"Jesus!" said Tommy. "Once they started hitting, I thought they'd never stop. And then, when all seems lost, Honus puts on the Superman cape!"

"Yeah, Honus – what a great play!"

"Hell, I had to make up for the one before. What was I thinkin'?"

"You were thinkin' about your family jewels," said Gilly. "God, I hate those grass-burners."

"Well I hate Los Tigres Assholes worse," I said. "And we beat 'em!"

But even in the glow of victory I could feel the shadows. Ever since the team re-formed, I had been pushing for a move to the Sunnyvale leagues. I was tired of the fight, tired of working so hard to defuse the machismo, and exhausted from trying to find a home.

The rest of the team was more determined than ever to conquer Double River – and they were getting stupid, in a desperate, aggressive sort of way. The ringleader was Greg Macy, whose home-run prowess had turned him into one of those dreaded Double River regulars. All of a sudden he seemed to know everyone at the complex, and I suspected he might be on a couple of those all-star teams that whooped up on lower divisions.

The widening gap was distilled by a single play the month before. I was on second, Tommy was on first. The next batter hit a line-drive single, but I had to freeze to let it pass in front of me. The basecoach spotted my hesitation and held me up at third. But Tommy, hearing the standard blood-thirsty screams from Greg and his monkeys in the dugout, put his head down and charged for third. When I saw Tommy coming to join me, I decided I had to at least force them to make a play, so I dashed for home, where the catcher tagged me out.

When I stood up to brush myself off, I could already read the vibes from the dugout. I had made three smart baserunning decisions in the course of ten seconds, and yet all they were thinking was, *If only Honus had run home in the first place, none of this would have happened.* That really pissed me off, and I let Greg know about it as I passed him in the on-deck circle.

"Why don't you shut the fuck up, Macy, and let the goddamn basecoach do his job?"

I immediately felt bad, because you should never cuss out someone who's getting ready to bat. I made a point of apologizing to him after the game, but I got a curious response.

"Actually, I had no idea what you were talking about – so hey, no biggie."

Was I speaking Russian out here? I wanted my apology to count for something, dammit. I wanted to make contact with someone on this team that suddenly seemed like a bunch of strangers.

As for Tommy, the one person in this scenario who actually owed someone an apology (namely, me), he just grumbled to himself after the third out and made his way to the pitcher's mound, as if the whole incident was just another brick in his personal wall of martyrdom. I had become invisible.

I was working at the cybercafe in Santa Clara when I got an email from Todd, the bike-park designer in Boulder Creek.

> *I'm really sorry to be writing this to you, but Emma's sister and brother-in-law are moving here from Texas, and it looks like they'll be living with us. I certainly apologize if this causes you any inconvenience. Please send me a mailing address and I will return your deposit check.*

Todd, I wrote back. *I cannot accept your apology, because this is not forgivable. And yes, it will cause me a hell of a lot of inconvenience. This is the rudest, most inconsiderate thing I have ever heard of.*

I was pissed, frustrated, and exhausted. That night, when I reported to my lead singer's house for rehearsal, I was clutching for straws.

I had spent my entire band career playing drums behind singers who couldn't sing as well as I could. This happens because good drummers are hard to find, whereas wannabe singers are hanging out on every streetcorner. Carly, the singer for our blues band, had a decent voice, but at the age of forty she was still in the beginning phases of learning how to use it. She had little understanding of phrasing and dynamics, sang in a narrow, five-step range, and had about as much soul as vanilla ice cream with marshmallow topping.

To her credit, Carly understood how much she needed to learn, and was open to my suggestions. But her insecurity led her to construct a barbed-wire fence around the vocals. She decreed that 80 percent of our set list would feature her on lead vocals, and the rest of us would split the remaining 20. My two songs were "Mustang Sally" and "I've Got You Under My Skin."

"My voice is my instrument," she would say. "When I'm not singing, I have nothing to do."

Sit down and have a friggin' martini, I thought.

I funneled my frustration into a jazz-duo act with my lead guitarist, Jon. We worked up a set of standards like "Skylark," and "Beyond the Sea," and made plans for some coffeehouse gigs.

We told Carly about this, but we were intentionally vague about our repertoire. We knew if we mentioned actual songs, Carly would glom on to them like a fungus and, what's more, sing them badly. That Tuesday night, however, I was feeling reckless. When Carly asked if she could try one of our tunes, I surprised Jon by suggesting "Fly Me to the Moon." She sang it horribly, but seemed to enjoy herself. And then I got myself a bad case of hubris.

"I was thinking," I said, sipping a beer afterward. "Since this jazz stuff is music that Jon and I have been working on, if we bring it into the band, I'd like to do a couple more vocals."

Carly's face went stiff as a mannequin.

"The music doesn't belong to you, Honus. And you know, we all agreed to an eighty-twenty ratio on lead vocals."

"We never agreed to that, Carly. You commanded that. And now I'd like to change that." *I'm drowning here, Carly. I'm reaching for one good thing from this shithole of a month.*

"My voice is my only instrument, Honus. When I'm not singing, I have nothing to do."

I don't trust men who say they don't have tempers. The men you trust are the ones who acknowledge their tempers, who make friends with their tempers, and know how to deal with them. Think of a pitcher who punches a wall with his throwing hand. Faulty temper management.

My explosions come once, twice a year. That morning, after Todd's weasely email, I drove to the far corner of the parking lot, rolled up the windows and screamed every swear word I could think of while I pounded the shit out of my well-cushioned dashboard. And here I was, six hours later, about to use up my annual allotment of temper tantrums in a single day. I looked at Carly's goddamn stone-face and thought of all the things I could tell her to do with herself while she wasn't singing. Instead, I stood from my drums, my blood fizzing with nitrogen, and left the house, giving the door a good percussive slam.

I walked to the corner in a daze and sat on the curb, curious drivers giving me the once-over from the stop sign. I wanted to cry, but I was too defeated and angry. Every goddamn person in the world had locked themselves up in trunks of thick steel. The only thing you accomplished by exposing your desperation was to drive them further inside. Altruism was a pleasant fiction spread by politicians and priests. We were all on our own.

All this thinking did nothing but wear me down even further. By the time I felt ready to re-enter the house (to retrieve my forgotten car-keys), I was a walking corpse. I sat limply on the couch to receive additional helpings of Carly's selfishness.

"When you slammed that door, Honus, you really hurt me. That sound hurt me worse than anything you could ever say to me."

I rubbed my eyes and tried to assemble a sentence.

"You wouldn't have wanted me to stay, Carly. So I left. I went somewhere to cool off. That's what I do."

"I just don't understand why you're so angry at me, Honus."

Turn the key, throw it away. My new world view had just been confirmed. I passed a note of apology to Carly, ten feet back in her steel vault, lugged my drums out to her tool shed, then drove off to my sister's camper. The world was composed entirely of containers, but not a one to call home.

The next day, I got a campsite at Sunset Beach, where I walked the shoreline singing "Help Me," an old back-porch blues that seemed a good match for my stride. Come Friday morning, the ranger told me they were full for the weekend.

I packed up my possessions and headed out, once again homeless. My cleats were literally bursting at the seams, so I headed into Sunnyvale for replacements. This being August, baseball cleats were not in ready supply. After scouring three stores, I settled for a pair of football shoes that seemed to do the job. So it was that I ventured into the evil baylands of Double River, beset by a macrame of anxiety, running on nothing but a single fast-food cheeseburger.

In the second inning, Tommy started yelling. An hour later, I returned for the windbreaker, he extended the invitation, I took it.

Walking around with half a ton strapped to my back, the chance to remove the hundred pounds represented by the Barons and their prickly manager was too good to pass up. I left Double River for the lovely state decals of my sister's camper and slept soundly till sunrise.

A week later, I asked my big sister what her husband Barry thought about my sudden departure.

"Actually, he's a little disappointed – and surprised. It didn't seem right for you to leave in the middle of the season like that. It also didn't seem... characteristic."

"Believe me," I said. "I had my reasons. I could not possibly have done anything else. I'm sorry for leaving them in the lurch. But to explain the whole thing… it would take a novel."

TWENTY-SIX

The Final Pitch

The great thing about friends is that you choose them. This sounds very cozy and uplifting, but it carries a fierce underbelly: you can also choose to get rid of them. In fact, the timely discarding of friends is one of the keys to a well-lived life.

Jerry was younger than me, and less educated. He worked in construction, and yearned to stretch his thoughts beyond his blue-collar milieu. Gradually, he developed an inferiority complex. This antipathy also showed up in our racquetball games. He was clearly the better player, but even if he lost a single game out of five he would fly into a self-flagellating rage. I began to call him less often. He accused me of being a snob for not calling him. I stopped calling him.

I met Esteban on a soccer team when I was twelve. We spent our high-school years pursuing girls, parties and ill-gotten booze. After graduation, we took different routes: mine to college and writing, his to a profession, a wife, a kid, and divorce. Years later, I visited him in Texas, where he lived with his second wife. I found that we still liked each other, but had nothing to talk about but high school. I passed through Texas two years later, but didn't bother calling.

Bob was my best friend from college. He married a harsh woman who ran his life for him – which is exactly what he wanted. I was uncomfortable with this, and drifted away. A few years later we reconnected, and I proposed writing a column for his paper. He expressed interest, and suggested we discuss it over lunch. When I brought it up at lunch, he said he had known all along the idea for the column was out of their jurisdiction. "Then why did you say you were interested?" I asked. "Because otherwise you wouldn't have had lunch with me," he said. Three kids later, he still hadn't grown up. I see him once a year, for lunch.

Savage business, this winnowing of friends. But it honors the friendships you keep, and it makes room for other possibilities. The week I gave up my friendship with Tommy Folgett and my place on the legendary Barons, those possibilities arrived in due haste. I found a room in a gorgeous two-story house in Los Gatos, presided over by a lovely divorced lady who looked like Sophia Loren and spoke with just a touch of a Bronx accent.

My next concern was keeping up with the rent, but this vanished within a week. I was hired by a friend of my sister's to paint two flood-damaged houses next to the Stanford University golf course. I was flush with cash through New Year's, and I worked in a beautiful, pastoral setting. I even made enough to get a new transmission for my sexy old sportscar.

I had a glorious autumn. I woke to the sound of horses headed for the riding trails across the street, then watched children playing at the pre-school behind us through the shower window. I Rollerbladed downhill through wild bursting clouds of gingko and Chinese pistache trees to write at the same cafe (a midpoint between my new place and Tommy's). I arrived home each night and sat on a bench between Greek Revival columns, charting constellations over the lightless foothills.

When I got the invitation to Shauna and Gilly's wedding, I guess I was a little surprised. I assumed my desertion had taken me out of the loop. I was also a little troubled. Much of the team would be there. Tommy would be there. It was bound to be uncomfortable. But what can you do? Someone invites you to their wedding, you go.

It was at a golf course (where else?) in the south San Jose hills. I drove through fields of grass gone the color of toast, and live oaks straddling the ridges like respected emperors. Or legendary Barons.

The ceremony took place at a flower-strewn archway behind the 18th green. The prenuptial music was "Take Five" by Dave Brubeck and "Freddie Freeloader" by Miles Davis, which I thought was just incredibly cool. I sat in my folding chair and spotted a great white heron splitting the sky – then turned to find my sister joining me. This shouldn't have surprised me – her husband was, after all, a Baron. In all my anxiety, the connection had slipped my mind. I was grateful to have someone I could talk to without watching my words.

The ceremony was brief and graceful, capped by comedy. Just as bride and groom were completing their vows, a golf ball bounded up on the green behind them, followed by a golf cart of old Japanese men wearing puzzled expressions.

I settled with my sister and brother-in-law at a table near the back of the reception hall. Eventually I worked up enough courage to head outside, where Stevie Hammer and Greg Macy were hanging out in their tuxedos with Johnny Silva and family. They seemed mystified at my presence, but glad to see me. After a round of friendly but cautious greetings, I returned to my table to find Stevie Becker and Tammy. Sitting in the chair next to mine was Tommy Folgett.

Tommy seemed just as dedicated to the spirit of the occasion as I was, and for quite a while we danced around the particulars of our recent past. I can't recall if my sudden departure even came up, but if it did, I'm sure that I was strategically vague in my response, reassuring Tommy that there were a dozen issues besides our personal frictions that led to my decision. Tommy's mind was on bigger issues, too, some of the "personal shit" he had alluded to that same night.

"I hadn't wanted to be too specific about it, Honus, but I had a tumor. It turned out to be benign, but anytime you hear the 'C' word, it really knocks you for a loop, especially when you've been abusing your body as long as I have.

"I've been spending this month cutting down on pot, drinking, smoking… coffee. I'm not about to fuck around with my health anymore. And I'm selling the house and moving to Florida, where my mom lives. It's a good time to get away from all the stress of the Valley."

"It sounds like just what you need, Tommy. You've been talking about Florida for a long time."

Tommy turned his steely blues to the end of the hall, where they were wheeling in the cake. "I got a free pass this time, Honus. A warning shot over the bow. If that doesn't scare you into changing, nothing will."

My sister and Barry excused themselves soon after dinner to get home to the kids. I wasn't long in following. I went to the head table to congratulate Gilly and dance with Shauna. I returned to say goodbye to Stevie and Tammy, then shook Tommy's hand and said, "Take care of yourself."

I went to my car and returned with one of the frosted glass mosaics I had fashioned in researching my novel. Just to make sure they understood my artistic intentions, I set it atop a hollow pedestal, equipped a small lamp that would shine up through the bottom. Then I headed outside, descending the broad steps of the clubhouse.

The setting and the warm evening demanded al fresco driving, so I took the panel from my T-top and let the air rush around my shoulders. It occurred to me that dropping a friend who had just had a cancer scare might be seen as a harsh act, but cold logic was on my side. Tommy Folgett could have been in perfect health that night and still been an asshole – and Double River was still a shithole. I would have been utterly miserable if I hadn't wiped the slate clean. It was the perfect time for an ending.

Wrap-Up

I couldn't have known that my second and third novels would soon be published – that I would finally feel comfortable calling myself an "author." But the smaller, sooner things were plenty. My Sunnyvale team won the championship. I was hitting to right again, hitting .700 again, once more hurling my body around left field with luxurious abandon. For the last out of the championship game, I chased a foul fly to the cypress bushes surrounding the light pole, timed my steps and jumped, picking the ball off the top like a migrant worker plucking an apple.

A year later, I am finishing this book when Shauna and Gilly roll up to the cafe in their SUV. Gilly is still buffed, Shauna still radiant, and their baby daughter, Brejenae, is extraordinarily cute. Heredity works.

"I heard Stevie Hammer is still heading up a Barons team," says Gilly. "But ya know, I can't handle that Double River stuff anymore. I've got too much to lose now, I can't be fighting over stupid little softball games. I think Macy feels the same way."

All that terrible summer, I thought I was the only one. Apparently I was just the first to express it.

A couple weeks before, I was out Rollerblading, and found myself in Tommy Folgett's neighborhood. It was a sunny autumn afternoon, the sycamores and birches blurting out color like that day at Tommy's garage sale.

When I rolled up to the old house I found the liquidambar a storm of russet, loaded with spiked dingleberry pods. The house itself was not quite so lovely; the new owners had painted it a combination of beige and bright green that would have made Tommy go blind. I rolled back to peek at my old bedroom, and found that the window was still cracked.

A few blocks later, I tried an old game. Rollerblade under a tree, catch a falling leaf – get a wish! A red sliver wafted down from a pistache and fell into my hand as easy as an infield fly. I usually wished for a Pulitzer, but not this time. This one went to Tommy Folgett – that wherever he was, he was doing well.

Also by Michael J. Vaughn

A painful break-up/break-down chases high-tech marketing wiz Sandy Lowiltry from her Silicon Valley home. She comes to rest on the Oregon Coast, where she seeks solace in the opera-themed sanctuary of the Hotel Bel Canto and the arms of a handsome eccentric who spends his days combing the beach for sea glass.

Sandy soon learns what the tourist ladies already know – it's easy to fall for Frosted Glass Man. Besides great sex and alarmingly intricate campsite cuisine, Frosty offers do-it-yourself mythologies that would melt even the coldest heart. But will it be enough to quiet the whisper of ambition, the voice inside Sandy's head that chides her for settling? Will she really leave behind Silicon Valley for love in such a strange package?

"…a most unlikely tale of discovery and passion. …a shimmering fable, as delicate and whimsical as a handful of glass."
– Debra Bokur, *Many Mountains Moving* literary journal

"A breezy, richly-textured romp through the inner circuitry of a postmodern heroine."
– Christina Waters, PhD, *Metro* Newspapers (San Jose)

…available everywhere books are sold…

As special thanks for purchasing this title,
we present an excerpt from FROSTED GLASS:

Far away, in the birthplace of music and strawberries, there lived a race of beings with skins of glass. Not the brittle, breakable glass of Earth, but a kind of self-contained fluid, a substance that could heal almost immediately after being scratched or punctured. Their organs were made of metals – soft, living versions of silver, copper and titanium. In order to hide these organs from view, their skin had developed an opaque, frosted appearance, much like Earth glass that has been tumbled in the ocean.

Because of these differences in their physical makeup, these glasslings lived much longer than humans, and were a highly evolved, creative race. Their greatest creativity came from their women, whose powers reached their peak during a psycho-physiological phenomenon known as a "blossomfire." Considered events of great awe and mystery, blossomfires would begin appearing in glass women at the age of maturity – about a thousand Earth years – and would cease at the age of reverence, around 4,300 years. Blossomfires usually appeared every 200 years, and lasted only a few Earth days – in glassling terms, a very brief period. Occasionally, however, there came a glass woman who carried the capacity for much lengthier blossomfires; one who was able to cultivate heightened powers and ever-expanding levels of creativity.

Just such a being was Frosted Glass Woman, who for purposes of this telling we will call "Sandy." Sandy's first blossomfire lasted for three of our weeks. As she matured into young womanhood under the tutelage of a woman of reverence we shall call "Lowiltry," her blossomfires lengthened into months and years, and her creative ventures grew ever larger and more complex. Her first was a process for distilling the elements of individual personalities into the form of perfumes. Her second was a kind of jewelry that changed shape and color according to the direction, intensity and pattern of a person's gaze. Another time, she invented a form of music that she called "jazz," but she had no idea what to do with it.

Nearing an age of 3,000 Earth years, Sandy realized that her powers were coming to a peak. For her next blossomfire, she settled on an unprecedented project: the creation of her own world. Her mentor, Lowiltry, warned against this. A project this expansive would extend Sandy's blossomfire to dangerous lengths. Those attempting this kind of extension before had fallen into a state the glasslings referred to as "the hardening," in which the fluid glass of the skin becomes hard and fragile like the glass of Earth. The condition lasted for a thousand years, during which time the victim had to be hung by wires over a bed of snowy egret feathers.

Shortly after this warning, however, Lowiltry was overcome by a sudden illness and began to rapidly deteriorate. At the very start of her student's Great Blossomfire, she passed away, her elements rising to the sky in banners of copper, silver and white vapor. Spying this sad but lovely vision as she entered her creative trance, Sandy was more determined than ever to achieve her ends, if only as a tribute to her mentor.

Dipping a hand into the glassling world's still-molten third moon, Sandy drew out a sphere of hot elements and blew it cool with her breath. As the crust began to harden she drew canyons and mountains with her fingers, and then outlined long gouges and wide depressions that she filled with her tears. She plucked out strands of her hair and formed them into trees, plants and seaweed, then molded small bits of the crust into mammals, fish and birds, animating them with drops of perspiration. She also found places for her previous inventions. The perfume she swept into the hearts of a million flowers. The jewelry she deposited just under the surface, where they awaited the wandering gaze, the searching hands. As for jazz, she hid that in the trunk of a tree on the plains of Africa.

Sandy completed her new world just as she felt her Great Blossomfire ending. But her creation was missing something, and she knew that this was something not even she could produce: living spirits, souls, intellects, sparks of self-knowledge. She felt great sadness, for what good was this new world of hers without some form of cognizant being to behold, observe and admire its beauty?

By the time she came to terms with her defeat, it was too late – the hardening had begun. Sandy felt great, sudden terror, not at the physical reality of her petrifying skin, but at the thought of spending year upon year suspended by wires as her creation sat there with no knowledge of its own existence.

Stumbling along on her stiffening limbs, Sandy drew herself down a path behind her home to the top of a great sea cliff. By the time she approached the edge, she could move only her left arm. But this was enough. With painful effort she pulled her green arms and face, her white torso and brown legs alongside the drop. She lifted her blue eyes in a final prayer to Lowiltry, then pushed off as her arm froze into place. Frosted Glass Woman hurtled avenues of air and fell to the rocks, smashing her skin into a million pieces.

Aware of their daughter's wishes, Sandy's bereaved parents spent the next three hundred years roaming the shoreline, gathering the pieces of their daughter's skin and scattering them over her newly created world. As the pieces became more and more difficult to find, and finally disappeared completely, her father became overwhelmed by grief. One morning, in a burst of anger, he picked up his daughter's world and hurled it into the vast recesses of space. The new world settled into orbit around a small, stable sun, and the pieces of glass took physical form, becoming that which we call women.

To this day, Frosted Glass Man wanders the shorelines of Earth, hoping one day to reassemble Frosted Glass Woman and bring her back to life.

Also by Michael J. Vaughn…

GABRIELLA'S VOICE

A NOVEL

MICHAEL J. VAUGHN

Fifty-year-old Bill Harness is on a strange seemingly benign journey, rambling across the coun in an old Pontiac and anonymously leaving la checks with promising young opera singers. His f however, is sorrow, and it isn't until he arrives o small island outside of Seattle and befriends Gabric Compton, a phenomenally talented soprano, that he able to address the three great tragedies of his voca gifted family.

"Michael J. Vaughn has turned out a beautiful, lyrical novel. I was caught in the narrative within three sentences and was held spellbound by the ste until the end. It is as captivating as a well-performed *La Boheme*, as tragic a triumphant as *Tosca*."

– Ani Harrison, *Tacoma Repor*

"By turns rousing, lyrical and intoxicating, GABRIELLA'S VOICE is the we of a virtuoso."

– Calder Lowe, *The Montserrat Revi*

"Vaughn performs the… task of invoking sounds from the silence of words paper. Arias whirl from the pages… a treat for the ear as well as the mind."

– Gregory Harris, *BookP*

…available everywhere books are sold…

Dead End Street® also highly recommends this title:

Suzanne Rosewell is the youngest female partner in the history of her prestigious Wall Street law firm. She's a strong, driven woman with  the will to succeed. Then she meets Elias Garner, an enigmatic black Jazz musician who carries an ancient golden trumpet and represents the even more furtive "Chairman" (whom we learn heads the most powerful corporation on earth).

Elias explains that God has always placed among us thirty-six righteous people – each of whom "knows the divine will" and all of which must be accounted for if humanity is to redeem itself. Five are missing from the Chairman's list and Suzanne is asked to set aside her career to search for them. If she is unsuccessful, it appears that the world cannot exist beyond the sunrise.

...available everywhere books are sold...

ANOTHER FINE OFFERING FROM

DEAD END STREET®

www.ingramcontent.com/pod-product-compliance
Lightning Source LLC
Chambersburg PA
CBHW050748250626
47155CB00005B/1967